DATE DUE

APR 15 '95			
MAY 6 '95			

Books by Barbara Morgenroth

RIDE A PROUD HORSE

LAST JUNIOR YEAR

TRAMPS LIKE US

IMPOSSIBLE CHARLIE

DEMONS AT MY DOOR

WILL THE REAL RENIE LAKE PLEASE STAND UP

IN REAL LIFE, I'M JUST KATE

IN REAL LIFE
I'm Just Kate

IN REAL LIFE
I'm Just Kate

Barbara Morgenroth

ATHENEUM   *1981*   New York

LIBRARY OF CONGRESS CATALOGING IN PUBLICATION DATA

Morgenroth, Barbara.
   In real life I'm just Kate.

   Summary; When her father is suddenly written out of
the TV soap opera in which he's long been starring,
seventeen-year-old Kate takes over as the family bread-
winner by acting in the same soap.
   [1. Actors and actresses—Fiction. 2. Family problems
—Fiction] I. Title.
PZ7.M82669In   [Fic]   81-1421
ISBN 0-689-30851-5   AACR2

DEDICATED to Denise Alexander, Genie Francis, Anthony Geary, Chris Robinson
and
Rick Anderson, Gerald Anthony, Jaime Lyn Bauer, Asher Brauner, Steve Carlson, Cindy Carol, Malcomb Coombes, Jacqueline Courtney, Joe Gallison, Kathy Glass, Bill Hayes, Susan Seaforth Hayes, Allan Miller, Julie Montgomery, Rick Moses, Kate Mulgrew, Lee Patterson, Jameson Parker, Tristan Rogers, Gillian Spencer, Yale Summer, Jacklyn Zeman.

Acknowledgments

I would like to thank Richard Van Vleet (CHUCK TYLER, AMC) for his much appreciated and invaluable help. I would also like to thank Gaile A. Burnell, assistant producer of ALL MY CHILDREN, as well as Tricia Pursley (DEVON SHEPPARD MCFADDEN), Larry Strack and the cast and crew for allowing me to see how a daytime serial is made.

IN REAL LIFE
I'm Just Kate

One

My FATHER DIED September 26, at 1:41 P.M.

Unconscious for about two weeks, even the efforts of the masterful surgeon, MILES FERGUSON, could not save him. He had been beaten unmercifully by a band of thugs employed by mob boss, LOUIE QUARANTELLO, who had been unable to reason with my father for his silence. So LOUIE had my father bumped off in an alley.

Off camera, of course. The censors don't allow much violence on camera anymore.

My father had been laid up with a subdural hematoma for two weeks, and as a result of various complications, septicemia for one, he was deep-sixed.

Not that we hadn't expected it. His contract had expired, but we had expected up until the end that the producers and my father's agent, Sylvia Greenburg, would renegotiate terms to everyone's satisfaction. But sure enough, it didn't go through; the last minute miracle wasn't delivered by the head writer, and my father died.

I watched. I didn't usually watch the daytime serials. (That's the class name. To me, they're still just soap operas.) But that day we gathered around the television set and watched my father in his death throes. He just died. He didn't even act. An intern (under five lines) came in when the heart machine straightlined and said, "He's dead." The end. Go to commercial.

Then it was really final, even though he had technically been out of work for two weeks, since LIFE TO ITS FULL-

3

EST—or LTIF as it's written on top of the scripts—is about two weeks ahead in the can. If that's what they call it for videotape. I never found out what else it could be called.

We sat there, shocked and devastated and wondering how we were going to pay for this big, beautiful house in the sub-suburbs when my dad was now unemployed. He had gone from commercials to a couple of different soaps and had wound up with LTIF, where he had been a regular for five years.

How they could have killed him off so easily is beyond me. One thing's for certain, the producers hold no loyalty to actors.

Everyone knows what kind of money soap actors get. Plenty. Yet we didn't have but a few cents in the bank. We had half the house, the bank had the other half. We had a big gas-guzzling Mercedes with the vanity license plates spelling R-A-F-R-T-Y.

That's our name. Rafferty.

My name's Kate.

You probably know me as Kathleen Rafferty, if you know me at all. And you might. The publicist at the network says I'm quite famous. The personality magazines say I'm very popular. My personal manager says I'm destined for big things and this is just the beginning. I'm developing a high TV-Q.

But I know differently. The real beginning was September 26, at 1:41 when DEREK SIMMONS died at Riverford Hospital, and Kerwin Rafferty hit the skids.

That day my mother and father turned to me as the credits rolled over the beauty shot and something clicked. I was now a marketable commodity. I was going to hit the boards. I was going to support the family.

Just until Dad got back on his feet, of course.

Since then the word temporary has gone out of my vocabulary. I will never believe anyone who just says I'll be committed to something for only a little while. I want everything in writing, in black and white, in language I can understand. And I want to know how much money I'm going to get.

But that's now.

On September 26, I was very stupid and too dumb to have reservations. Or too young to know better. It always surprises me how much older I got within a few months.

It's one of my policies not to trust anyone. I don't even trust my manager, who gets twenty percent of everything I make just to take care of me. For that twenty percent, there is enough greed in Sylvia that she will sell me out if the money is right. When agents smile, their teeth drip blood. That's just a fact of life.

That's why I pay a lawyer to watch Sylvia and make sure she's not ripping me off, at least not too badly.

But that's business, and I don't spend much time thinking about it. I have practically a battalion of people who are supposed to watch each other and squeal on the first guy who steps out of line.

There is nothing of art in acting, it's all business.

That's probably the first lesson I learned.

Not that I ever wanted to go into show biz. I know how it seems to run in families. Ed Wynne, his son Keenan Wynne and the grandson Tracy Keenan Wynne. John Wayne and Patrick Wayne. Judy Garland and Liza Minelli. Gene Lockhart, June Lockhart and Anne Lockhart. And we mustn't forget America's first family of acting, the Barrymores. The list is almost endless.

Listen, I know. I was brought up in show biz, or on its fringe. From the time I was small, everyone assumed I would follow in my father's footsteps. He was so good-looking; and luckily, I took right after him. Not that my mother isn't an attractive lady, she's just not striking in the way my father is.

He's Irish. The Black Irish strain. Everyone thinks the

Irish all have red hair, but that's not true. Some have very dark hair. Maybe when the Spanish Armada came sailing north, they took a side trip to Ireland to mingle for a while before they engaged the British in sea warfare.

Whatever, I do resemble my father, for which I suppose I should be grateful. It put me where I am today.

Where that is exactly, I'm not quite sure.

I don't know where I'm going, but I'm making good time.

Two

"WE'RE GOING to the city tomorrow," my mother announced.

"Why?"

"Because we have appointments."

I didn't like the sound of that, and I didn't know what it meant. There were no appointments I could have in the city, and I wasn't very fond of the city anyway. I refused to take the subway. I was always afraid I was either going to fall onto the tracks or be pushed. My mother always went to the very edge of the platform, inviting disaster, to see if the train was coming.

To see if the train was coming? Please. You could hear the train coming long before you could see it, but still my mother would always lean over the track and peer into the tunnel. She's a crazy person, and I refuse to go on the subway.

I'm not wild about buses, either. I'm afraid the doors will close on me before I get off. I don't mean they will shut in front of me; I mean they will actually close on me, squeezing me between them. I heard that happened once, and it bothers me.

Taxicabs are all right; but they're too expensive, so I'm morally against them.

Of course, when my father was working, we had enough money to take taxicabs all around New York. We could live like the near rich, the rich and the super-rich.

All of which accounts for why we never had money in the bank.

"What kind of appointments?" I asked.

My mother walked through the living room into the kitchen, which meant I had to follow her. "Sylvia Greenburg for one."

I was instantly suspicious. "Which one of us does Sylvia want to see?"

It wasn't that I didn't like Sylvia; she was an old family friend, but I won't say I trusted her. She was tough and brassy and had always pinched my cheek. I hadn't seen her in about a year because the last time she had come up to the country for a weekend visit at our house, I had stayed with Marcia Loesch, my best friend.

"You, of course," my mother replied.

That was no surprise. Sylvia had been harping about getting me into the business ever since I was a baby. Such a sweet face and those eyes. Brother! Sylvia could really drive me to the brink of disgust with all the fussing over me.

I had always thought Sylvia was really more interested in my father, but couldn't very well say what a sweet face he had and those eyes! Phew! So she fussed over me.

I knew it was useless, but I decided to try to get out of it. "I don't want to see her."

"Too bad. We have a lunch date, and we're going."

At least I had registered my opinion. "So where else do we have to go?" I asked sitting down at the kitchen table.

I could understand my parents' panic. We had a magnificent home, a restored farmhouse with a pond, a sweeping view, and deer running through the yard eating all the plants. It was like a park, or the estate of rich people. So I knew it was more than one step up for my parents, neither of whom had had it so good when they were young.

The kitchen was every woman's dream. Or so *House and Garden* would have you believe. They had done an article on actors' country homes, and ours had been the one featuring the kitchen with the brick floor, the brick wall complete with the original and quaint dutch oven (quite useless when the

8

Jenn-Air was ten feet away), a fireplace, and every modern gleaming convenience.

I wouldn't want to throw all of this over if I could help it, either. If I was my mother.

As for my father, I didn't know. He was sorely wounded (his words) by his betrayal at LIFE. He had to take a rest and recover from his terrible ordeal.

All that translated to the fact that he had turned down every one of Sylvia's suggestions for work. He might have been able to go to another soap, but he wouldn't even go into the city and talk about it. All he did was stay in the living room (sunken, four steps down) and play the piano most of the day. When he wasn't wandering aimlessly around the house.

"We have a ten o'clock appointment with Vincent at Jean Reynard."

"You can't be serious."

"I most certainly am."

And she was, too. She was ready to blow a hundred bucks on getting me a haircut and whatever all get-out they'd lay on me. Jean Reynard wasn't as visible as Sassoon or Suga, but he was the very posh hairstylist to the stars; and that in this business is a very important man. He works wonders, darling, just wonders.

I didn't need any wonders worked on me, at least I hadn't thought I did. I was very content just the way I was. I pulled my hair back into a braid so it stayed off my face and out of my mouth. I didn't goo up my eyelashes with mascara, and I didn't wear lipstick. I was just like an Ivory girl. I washed my face with soap and water, and that was it.

I didn't care what I looked like. Maybe that's easy for me to say, when I knew I wasn't bad looking whatever I did or didn't do. I just wasn't into spending a half hour every morning before school painting myself up to impress someone.

I wasn't interested in impressing anyone anyway. There was no one around to impress.

"I suppose I can't wear blue jeans."

"Of course not. You will wear something decent."

I wasn't very interested in clothes. That's why I was having trouble with the concept of being in show business. It was bizarre. People in show biz are interested in make-up, clothes, acting, performing and impressing people. I'd never been concerned with even one of those things.

Luckily, I had my mother there to guide me. She had been a model for a while (that was how she had met my father) and knew all about clothes. She made most of mine. And what she didn't make, I did. All except jeans. No one does it better than Levi's.

Getting dressed up for show business is an art. You have to convince people to want you. That's what it's all about. You have to make them WANT you. And I couldn't have cared less. But I knew my mother did. She'd take care of it all. She would make them *want* me, on my behalf.

"I want you to look sophisticated but not distant."

"You want me to look real?" I asked.

She was pressing her favorite silk blouse. "Reachable but just beyond grasp."

"Does that mean real?" There is a whole different language to show biz.

"In a sense. There has to be a certain quality there."

"Innocence?"

"Yes . . . but you'll never look completely innocent." Even she had to smile.

I knew what that was all about. I looked too much like a gypsy to be the girl next door.

"We have to be very careful with your image."

My image. That should have been the warning bell, but I let it go right by.

"After all, you just turned seventeen even if you do read older."

Read in that sense means "comes across."

"We want you to seem worldly, but delicate."

"Lolita was thirteen," I said.

"Lolita"—my mother said each syllable distinctly—"has no bearing on your career."

I had a career already, and I hadn't even left the house.

"I want you to get to sleep early so you look your best tomorrow."

"I guess that means I'm not going to school."

"That's right. If things work out, you won't be going there much longer."

I stood up. "Oh."

"I want you to look upon this as a great adventure."

I nodded. "Okay."

"Now get yourself upstairs and prepare for tomorrow."

I went up the back stairs (we had two sets of stairs in the house) and into my bedroom.

Maybe I was going to finish my senior year at a professional high school. Or maybe I was going to have a tutor.

What did my mother have in mind for me?

Probably some light commercial work. Hold a package of gum or something. Commercials bring in good money. When my father did the Fresh Spring Soda commercial, which ran over seven months, we were rolling in money.

I didn't know what else I could do but stand in front of a camera and smile. I had never acted in my life, except in a grade school pageant. I played a dahlia.

I couldn't learn lines. I didn't know how to do anything like that.

What I also didn't know was that I didn't have to know anything about it.

Three

I FELT COMPLETELY OUT OF PLACE as we walked into Jean Reynard's salon. The girls behind the receptionist's desk were like ads for a cosmetics company and looked from me to my mother to determine which of us was going to be put to rights.

We sat down on a couch to wait, and I picked up a magazine. It was in French. All the magazines were in French, so I had to be content with looking at the photos.

Then a tiny lady named Sarita came to take me into the back. I had to change into a robe, get my hair washed, and only then would I be ready for Vincent to cut my hair.

I sat in the chair, looking at myself with a towel wrapped around my head, and felt pretty miserable. There was my front in front of me as well as my back in front of me from the mirror on the opposite wall. The whole place was mirrors, geometrics and exotic palms. I knew I didn't belong there. Everyone else came through in minks and sables and fitch, with diamonds and gold baubles.

"Hold up your chin," my mother said, looking at me in the mirror.

I did.

"Look at that bone structure."

She'd been looking at that bone structure for seventeen years and it had never been worthy of comment before.

"If I had had those cheekbones, I would have had the career Suzy Parker did."

"Uh huh." All I could envision was walking away from

the salon resembling a newly shorn sheep. For the past six years I hadn't had anything done to my hair but trimmed. It was almost down to my waist. Braid or not, I liked it just the way it was.

Vincent strutted up to my chair and looked at me in the mirror. That's when I found that out. No one in that kind of place ever looks at you directly; they only look at you in the mirror. It doesn't matter that you're backwards that way, it's the way they want to see you.

He took a handful of my hair and frowned. "What do you want me to do with this?"

"Cut it," my mother said with the finality of an executioner.

Mentally I prepared to bare my neck and pray for better things in the hereafter.

"I don't know what you're trying to achieve."

"She's going to be working professionally and needs a new image."

Who says? What was wrong with my old image?

"We're going to leave it in your hands," my mother said smiling.

She had nothing to lose and could afford to trust him. But what if he suddenly went berserk with the scissors? What if he gave me the kind of haircut I had once seen on a New York bus? The woman looked as though a UFO had landed on her head.

Vincent pumped up the chair, then bent down so that his face was level with mine. He stared at me in the mirror.

"She's only just seventeen, but we'd like her to pass for a few years older; at the same time she should be able to look young, too. She's with Sylvia Greenburg, and we expect to get some TV work."

Vincent nodded slightly, still within an inch of my face.

This was all Sylvia's fault. She had probably asked for a Caribbean island when she tried renegotiating my father's contract. It was not her style to be reasonable, she just barreled through, no finesse. I decided as Vincent picked up a pair of scissors and lopped off about ten inches of hair in one clip that I was going to watch Sylvia very closely and make sure she didn't mess me up the way she had my father.

And I wasn't going to forgive her too quickly for this. Vincent lopped off some more hair, and I closed my eyes. I didn't want to watch.

He cut and cut then ran the blow dryer and still I didn't look at myself. I was scared. I knew I was going to look like someone else after he got through.

Then he put down the dryer and stopped dragging the brush through my hair.

"Oh Kate," my mother said. "Just look at yourself."

I looked up.

Sure enough there was someone else sitting in my chair.

Now there was a little crowd around me. All looking at me in the mirror. All amazed. All preening with the success of their handiwork.

"Someone find Mr. Reynard."

"Sarita, get some brown mascara and some umber shadow," Vincent commanded.

She thumped back in her four-inch high heels and began painting my face. With a device similar to the tongs my mother used to turn fried chicken, Sarita curled my lashes and darkened them. Just the tips she said.

Then Jean Reynard himself came to stand by my chair. There was a concert of bated breath. Would *El Exigente* speak?

"Ahh," he said.

Everyone smiled. I waited for flower petals to be thrown to the wind. I waited for them to bring on the dancing girls. I waited for some sign in my face that I recognized the girl in the mirror.

It was really astonishing. Kathleen Rafferty.

* * *

"Oh Diana, she's gorgeous!" Sylvia gushed as she rose from her seat in the restaurant and gave my mother a big hug. I didn't feel gorgeous. I felt like a little kid dressed up for Halloween, wearing her mother's wig and make-up and someone else's clothes.

Sylvia reached forward to give me my pinch but kissed me instead. "You certainly have grown up. I don't see you for a couple of months, and you bloom into a real beauty. But why have you been hiding yourself up in the country?"

I wanted to hide, to sit down and pull a huge menu in front of my face so no one would see me.

Fact was, there were more than a few people in the restaurant who were now looking at us. I hoped it was because Sylvia had a booming voice and they weren't looking specifically at me.

"Hi Sylvia," I said and sat down quickly. For years I had gone through life totally inconspicuous, and now because of a haircut and some paint, people were looking at me. On the way to the restaurant, three construction workers had whistled at me.

I didn't want people whistling at me.

There's a difference between being pretty good-looking (which I had known I was before) and capitalizing on it (which I hadn't done before). I wasn't the flamboyant type like my father; I wasn't interested in inviting people to pay attention to me. I didn't need mass affection.

Kerwin Rafferty relishes attention. There is nothing he enjoys more than playing the piano and hamming it up, whether it's for the family, a cocktail party or piano bar. He loves to perform and needs to have people watch him. And approve.

I wasn't a performer. There wasn't a thing I could do. I had had tap lessons and could just about manage to shuffle off to Buffalo without tripping myself. I had had ballet, and was the despair of my teacher. I had had piano lessons. So now I could read music, but I wasn't going to play for anyone. And sing? Well, I could carry a tune. But not in front of anyone.

I hadn't been in any school plays (except as the red dahlia whose petals shed through the entire scene), and I was as interested in embarking on an acting career as I was in journeying into the Everglades to test honey as a mosquito repellent.

It seemed to me that all actors had a burning desire to have outsiders approve of them. To me, it was a little like an incurable illness. I knew my father had caught the disease; but I was immune. I could live happily without any strangers cheering me on.

At the same time, I knew that if I didn't help my father out, he'd probably start crying. Oh brother! Actors are a different breed altogether. For one thing, you can't trust them. They can cry or laugh whenever the script calls for it. I didn't trust my father not to use whatever weapons he had in his arsenal to encourage me to make us some money while his career collapsed. Just to tide us over.

The real problem was that my father had hit the skids before, and these momentary setbacks were serious things with him. During a tough period when I was about ten, my father got shaky, and it took about a year for him to pull himself together. The memory of what life was like that year scared me enough that I wouldn't say no to any plan, just to keep him straight until he got ready to work again.

We ordered and sat back to wait for lunch. I had real food, Sylvia and my mother had salads. I guessed I'd be switching one of these days, too, although I didn't have to watch my weight. Someone might think I should.

"I've got you a three o'clock appointment downtown at Jerry Della Femina's. He's casting a commercial, some new candy bar aimed at the teenage market."

"Della Femina, he's the top man in the business," my mother told me.

"That's right," Sylvia replied. "Honey, I want you to make a good impression on him. Don't come on too sultry with him, he's looking for kids."

Sultry? "I'm a kid," I said.

"Honey, if you look at him the way you do when you're just a little bored, he'll think you're at least twenty-one. Come in bright and bouncy."

Bright and bouncy. Right, Kate. Can you remember that? And heaven forbid I should be bored; who knew where it would get me?

At least I wouldn't have to be a photographic model. Sylvia wasn't that kind of agent. It sounded horrible to stand in front of a lens all day.

"How did you get her an appointment with Della Femina without a composite?" my mother asked.

"We're pretty close, and he trusts me without photos. I said I had the perfect teenager for him, and he believed me. But I want you to go out and get shots right away. I'll need them to send around."

"Is Peter Carolingian still in the business?" my mother asked.

"Yes, and he's a good man. I think he'll like her." Sylvia was staring at me again. "Ummm. We have to find just the right place for her. We don't want to take just anything, it has to be right." Right was one of her favorite words.

"Don't forget, Sylvia, Kate's never acted."

That didn't faze her one bit. "We'll send her to Sandy Meisner if she needs help. But she looks like a natural to me."

How can you tell?

Sandy Meisner? It was pretty chummy calling Sanford Meisner "Sandy." He was one of the top dramatic coaches in the country. Probably the world. Not only did I not want acting lessons, Sanford Meisner probably wouldn't want me either.

Sylvia glanced toward her watch. "Woops! Dear, I've got to run." She stood. "Just one last thing. The ratings for LIFE have dropped terribly in the past few weeks. They're scrambling to put the show back on its feet, but they're having a tough time. It's third in its time slot, so I imagine it'll be moved, but they know they're in big trouble. Couldn't happen to nicer people, huh. I'll be in touch."

Sylvia kissed us both a hasty goodbye and left.

"Well, what do you think?"

I didn't think anything. It was all happening too fast. "Are you sure we aren't making some kind of mistake?"

"What kind of mistake?"

"Maybe you should be going out for commercials and not me. I can't act."

"Kate, you'll do just fine, but you have to have more confidence in yourself. It's called chutzpah. You have to believe you can do anything. Let's go. We have to get downtown to Della Femina's."

Right. Confidence. Chutzpah.

We took a cab. Obviously we were going to be living high even when we were broke.

Jerry Della Femina happened to be at his tiny hole in the wall studio that day. He took one look at me, put his hand under my chin and raised it.

"Pretty girl," he said thoughtfully to no one in particular. "But too exotic."

I didn't get the job.

Four

A COUPLE OF DAYS LATER I was in Gene DeMeglio's office, sitting uncomfortably in a modern chair, looking out the window. In the distance I could see Central Park.

I knew that one's proximity to Central Park was a measure of how successful or how important one was. If you were someplace around Twenty-Third Street, you were a real bum. But if you were on Central Park West, then you were Klass. Gene DeMeglio wasn't on Central Park, but from his office you had a good view of it from the south.

Gene DeMeglio was one of the producers of LIFE TO ITS FULLEST. Isn't that ironic. I mean, truly ironic. They kill my father; and two weeks later, I'm in show biz trying to get a job from the same Huns.

And it scared me. Sylvia blew it once with these people, and frankly, I didn't trust her to handle it this time.

I had read for a part on LIFE, and they adored me. Sort of.

Until you've been around these show biz types, you can't imagine how they gush at you. They don't do or say anything by half-measures. They *adore* you, they don't just like you. They *despise* the very air you breathe; then you're not suitable for the part. I was already negating most of what I heard.

Everyone knew LIFE was in serious trouble. It was when they started losing sponsors, that they really got scared. Panic time in year zero. Then the network put it to them; get that show number one in its time slot or the whole thing's cancelled.

Even in the new three o'clock position, it was flopping. So the writers and the producers decided to add some new characters to stir things up, some young people. Most of the cast had been with them for years and were dead, it was just that no one had told them yet.

So they were casting two teenage girl parts: The lush LOUISE's daughter, and get this, MILES FERGUSON's daughter by his first marriage. I had no preference.

FONDA, LOUISE's daughter by a Spanish count, was supposed to be a bad girl. That sounded fairly interesting.

Then there was RACHEL FERGUSON, who was supposed to be the sweet all-American-girl-next-door type whose nemesis was FONDA, or something like that. No one had really figured it out yet exactly. It was explained to me, but I had never understood what made these shows tick anyway.

What did I care? No matter which part I got, I'd still get paid; and all I would be doing was reading the lines. I wasn't going to get emotionally involved either way. It was finally decided that I would look best as RACHEL.

I did think my being considered for his old show hurt my father's feelings a little. But I told him that the writers could always write him back in, as his own twin. He could be DEREK SIMMON's long lost brother DIRK, who would turn up suddenly and might prove to be the real father of RACHEL FERGUSON. That way we'd be playing father and daughter. Believe it or not, that cheered my father right up. I think Dad was still a little angry with MILES FERGUSON for letting him die anyway, and any trouble visited upon the great surgeon would have pleased Dad.

"Gene, I think Kathleen would be a real shot in the arm to LIFE."

That was the beginning of Sylvia's pitch. I sat back and looked out at the city. I didn't like the city and really would have preferred to be at home in Mrs. Freuchtignicht's history class.

"What's good about Kathleen is that she can look young now, but in six months you can start maturing her if the story line calls for it, and you can introduce older material."

I had been to Jean Reynard that morning for a touch-up. I wasn't allowed to go for the interview as is. Vincent had even spoken to me this morning. He hadn't opened his mouth to me the first day. And Faith Hunter sat next to me.

You know Faith Hunter. She's the blonde who's been dating every eligible man in Hollywood for the past two years. She's not an actress; she just spends her life dating people. And appearing on talk shows.

Gene put up his hand. "You don't have to convince me, Sylvia; she's got the job. I love her. We'll be hiring several other young people, and I think she'll be just wonderful."

Great.

Then Gene told Sylvia how much I'd be getting. It was standard scale for the first weeks, and I would be guaranteed two days a week. I was praying that Sylvia would agree to it immediately without bringing any hostility into the room. I got lucky, and she kept her mouth shut.

I had the job.

Getting a job on a soap is the first rung on the ladder to stardom. You know that. We all know that. It's what the fan magazines tell us.

I was going to play RACHEL FERGUSON, and I was hoping that the great surgeon's daughter was going to give him plenty of trouble, which would be my small revenge for his letting DEREK SIMMONS die and forcing me, Kate Rafferty, the me of real life, to go out and get a job.

It was all explained to me before I even got near the studio, even before my mother and I trotted over to the AFTRA office, where for $300 initiation fee and six months dues of $23.75, I legally became a union member and eligible to work. LIFE had gotten very old, so they needed young people to attract a younger audience and bring up LIFE's ratings in the time slot. They figured it would take six months to make all the changes and get some momentum going.

Since MILES FERGUSON was already married and had a young son who had died, the only way they could bring in a grown daughter suddenly was to make her of the long-lost variety. It seemed that MILES had been married to RACHEL's mother, CONSTANCE, at a very young age, when he was just an intern. The marriage hadn't worked, they divorced after only a few months, and CONSTANCE moved away. She was pregnant with me, RACHEL; but, get this, never told MILES. (Some switch, huh? It sounded stupid to me, but since I wasn't going out for a job as a writer, I didn't care—as long as they didn't bump me off in the first six weeks.) When CONSTANCE dies in a car crash, RACHEL comes to Riverford to find her dear father.

This was all very spur-of-the-moment. Which translates to the network's having given the producer an ultimatum (get those ratings up NOW or your head and your body will be merely passing acquaintances.) So what could Gene do but pass the suggestion on to the head writer, David Dietz (you invent something fabulous within two weeks or you'd better learn to type with your toes). And presto, RACHEL FERGUSON.

I think they were all so scared at this point (even though they were all smiling quite calmly) that they were running like jackasses with their ears pinned back; but that's just a personal opinion. If not, why would they have hired a kid from Connecticut whose only acting experience had been as a flower. I figured I should just accept it as a fact that when these TV people are in trouble, they'll do anything to save their skins, even if what they do doesn't make much sense.

In a flurry of writing genius, all current story lines ground to an abrupt halt while new ones were brought in. That meant that instead of GENEVA wondering whether or not she was going to have the baby out of wedlock, an abortion, or marry JOHN even though he wasn't the father (at least he proposed), they sent her to Michigan to think about it, out of their way.

As for the Kate of real life, I was requesting that I be permitted to stay in school until Thanksgiving. I had asked for the end of the semester. No dice. Christmas. Nope. I knew I wasn't going to make it to Thanksgiving either. (Thank you very much.) It would be professional correspondence school.

None of the kids at my real school could understand my transformation. One day I had a braid down my back; the next I looked like a cover girl. They started treating me like someone they didn't know. Guys who formerly ignored me were now bumping into me, accidentally on purpose, in the hallways. It had nothing to do with me. It was just this concept they had of people who work on television, as it they were different somehow—wonderfully, magically—from everyone else. I hadn't changed. They had.

My best friend, Marcia, was delighted for me, for both of us. She loved reading *Daystars;* it was her favorite magazine, before *People* even. I couldn't explain why I thought it was all a big drag and would gladly have traded places with her.

"But it'll be so exciting," Marcia said as she sat on my bed and watched me putting things into a small tote bag for my first day of taping.

"It's work. A job."

"Have you been watching LIFE? NICK is the cutest guy on TV. Do you think you'll get to work with him? Directly, I mean."

I had already read a projection of what was going to happen in the next two weeks. That was as far as the writers had gotten. Subject to change without notice. "No." Everyone told me not to spill any secrets, but that wasn't much of a secret. "RACHEL has gone to a convent school and thinks men are creepy," I said.

"Really?" Marcia's mouth fell open in amazement.

I was kind of amazed myself. I had made that up. "No, it's only on the surface that she thinks men are bums. She's really crazy about them, and it was something she had to fight the nuns about all the time."

"Wow."

I made that up, too. No one had any idea what RACHEL was like before Day One in Riverford. "But I can't tell you any more, they made me sign an oath."

"Really? Wow."

No oath.

"Are we still going to be friends after you become famous?"

"Famous?" The idea was ludicrous. I was working to save the house and my father's dignity until he could get his own job. I didn't want to be famous, not that I had to worry about that. I was the girl who didn't even want to be an actress.

"I can see it all now. Kathleen Rafferty on the cover of *Daystars, People, Time*. The brightest young star of television, discovered on LIFE TO ITS FULLEST. Oh Kate, you're so lucky. Do you think you'll have a house in Bel Air or Malibu?"

"I was thinking about the Holmby Hills. I heard Cher's place is up for sale."

"Oh wow! Really?"

"Marcia! This is the real world. I have a very small part in a New York soap. I'm not going to the Coast to star in a feature film, and I'm not going to be a superstar. Try not to let your imagination run away with you, okay? And yes, we'll always be friends as long as you're not locked up in the fruitcake ward. Some of your ideas border on insanity."

"You just don't realize how far you can go."

"I realize how far you can go. Right off the deep end."

Besides, it would be infinitely bad manners to become a

star before my father. He'd been working at becoming a star for most of his life; and although he'd gotten plenty of work, he'd never made that big breakthrough. I thought it would just about kill him to have recognition come easier to me than it had to him.

I was very glad that that wasn't one of my worries.

Five

MY MOTHER HELPED ME learn my lines. I had thought, because I had never paid any attention to what my father was saying about his work, that people memorized lines. Some people do; but those people are not real, genuine, artist-type actors. That's what my father told me at dinner the night before the first taping. Real actors learn their lines, they know where the dialogue is going, and they can fudge if they go up, which means everything about them goes totally blank. Like shutting off the electricity. People who memorize go up all the time; and it's such a bad thing to do—going up that is—that it's practically a sin. Professionals make a habit not to get caught going up too frequently; they don't get caught because they've learned how to finesse their way around temporary amnesia regarding scripts.

So I learned the stupid lines; and they were stupid. The writers hadn't quite gotten the picture of what RACHEL was doing in Riverford, so they were literally winging it. My father said so as he tossed me the script, skimming it gracefully over the dining room table.

The next morning my mother and I got in the car while it was still dark. It wasn't even six o'clock yet, and we were on the road to the city. Since I was in the first act, since I was a beginner, and since we had run-throughs at 7:30, I had to leave early. Somehow I hadn't realized how early it was when my father left for work before I left for school; but it was the way things had always been. Now it seemed different and pretty terrible. I was half asleep on the drive down.

We passed the security guard and went upstairs to the rehearsal room where everyone met. They all looked half asleep and bleary-eyed. I figured I must have looked something like everyone else and decided not to look in a mirror to find out.

I sat down at a table, my mother beside me, and we opened the script.

"Okay, Hugh. You're going to be on the phone, talking, as the scene opens. As you hang up, there's a knock on the door. Kate, that's when you come in. When you say the line 'It's me, Dad, RACHEL.' see if you can't quiver your voice a little. Then you embrace."

Lavinia Dale-Crozier paced the floor in front of us. As the director, she would tell us what to do, right down to the last inch. There wasn't time for any discussion, and no one seemed to care much. In fact, everyone seemed pretty much still asleep. When I looked over to MILES FERGUSON's father, TRAVERS, the old gentleman was actually sleeping soundly.

I made notes on the script, trying to remember everything I was supposed to do and not do. For the first time on, I was in three scenes, which was more than I needed. I wanted to do well. I wanted to do it well enough so that I wouldn't make any waves.

I also had to do well enough to make sure my standard thirteen-week contract would be picked up in January for at least the next six months. By the end of that time maybe my father would be ready to take over as the talent in the family. Since I had made the commitment under a form of family duress, I wasn't going to complain or struggle; whatever these soap people might dish out, I was prepared to take. For about nine months. After that, I wanted to go back to being a civilian. I mean, I would have put in my time, made my contribution; then I figured I'd be a free woman.

We finished the script, and I looked up at the huge industrial clock. It read ten. We had fifteen minutes before going into the studio for the breakdown.

I don't think of myself as a shy person, but I'm not the type to go walking up to people with my hand out prepared for a stout shake. Everyone in the show that day was part of the old family. None of the other new people hired during the blitz were to appear yet and I felt very out-of-place in a group that laughed and talked and told private jokes. Some of the people I knew, because they had been out to the house for parties and such over the past five years; others I knew because I had seen them on the show. Yet it was as if I knew none of them. I told myself all beginnings are difficult and by the end of my thirteen weeks, we'd all be friends.

"Diana, how are you?" Grace Ransom said as we stepped out of the rehearsal hall.

"Fine. How are you and William?" my mother replied.

"Just fine. We spent our week this fall in Bermuda. It was lovely. I'm so glad you're with us now, Kathleen."

I nodded. Grace was an old friend. She played the mother of LISA, to whom DEREK had been married. In every serial there is either a mother or father confessor character, the voice of age and wisdom. Grace played VIOLET HEGARTY with over forty years of experience behind her. She was everyone's favorite grandmother.

"I was so sorry to see Kerwin go, even though DEREK was such a rat," Grace said laughing as we went downstairs. "What would LIFE be without a Rafferty?"

"I don't know," I replied.

"I'm sure you'll love it here; we have great fun."

I nodded again.

"I'm sure Kate will come to love it as much as you do," my mother replied.

Not so fast, Mom. I'll come to accept it, but love? That's a different matter.

I waited while my mother had a cup of coffee; then a

voice called over the intercom that we were all to go into the studio. We walked past the room where they handled the sound, and the control room with its wall of tiny television screens: some in black and white, some in color, some showing color bars, and one cut into four unequal sections. I knew something about all those screens. The one labeled LINE was the picture being taped. The one labeled PREVIEW was the picture coming next.

Years ago my father had the t.d. (technical director) show me how all the parts made up a whole show. There were three cameras. The t.d. would tell each cameraman what shot he wanted through a headset. When camera one came on, there was a red tally light on the camera, which told the actors what direction they were being seen from. The t.d. was able to move camera 2 and camera 3 while 1 was on. Then he might say over the headset for camera 1 to begin to pull back, and he'd take camera 2 forward to get his next shot.

So at all times the t.d. had three separate shots from different angles in front of him. With serials on videotape, there wasn't much time to go back and edit, make cuts and improve things. So the three-camera technique was supposed to make the finished product come out looking smooth and flowing. Considering that they made an hour show each day, it was something of a minor miracle that it all came out as well as it did. But there was no time even to edit out small mistakes, so when VIOLET called my father Kerwin instead of DEREK one day, they let it go by.

Also because they have to complete a show a day, every day, five days a week, there are always at least three separate units on the floor, not always the same ones, of course. With a minimum of equipment wheeling, a scene can be shot at one end of the studio and then another scene can be shot immediately at the opposite end. One minute's time is a huge amount and cannot be wasted, so things on the floor tend to roll with incredible speed.

Even so, the few times I had watched my father work, I had found it boring. He'd have a scene with three minutes of conversation, then sit fifteen minutes in silence waiting for another turn.

"Okay, RACHEL, you stand on the other side of MILES's door and wait for your cue," Lavinia told me.

MILES smiled.

"Is JANICE here?" Lavina called.

"I'm coming!" Miriam Stern called as she ran into the studio with a cup of coffee in one hand and about twenty curlers in her hair. It was freezing cold in the dark cavern they called a studio. Above me were a couple of hundred lights hanging on long rods running crosswise overhead. The ceiling was almost too high to see, maybe thirty or forty feet up; it was like a warehouse with corners of rooms stuck into it.

Somehow it all looked very different from the way it looked on television. Smaller. It was almost like stepping into Riverford, but a Riverford seen in a wavy carnival mirror. I recognized the FERGUSON living room, but where was the rest of the house?

I heard MILES begin his speech, his voice quickly swallowed up in the gut of the studio.

"Okay, RACHEL. MILES opens the door. You enter. Walk in to the edge of the carpet. Stop. Somebody! Give her a mark," Lavinia directed.

The a.d. (assistant director) took a roll of red tape from his pocket, ripped off a strip and placed it in front of my foot on the brown tile floor.

"MILES close the door, take two steps and stop. Give him a mark. RACHEL your turn. Say your line."

"It's me, Dad. RACHEL." I said.

"MILES be caught by surprise. Then take two steps. Embrace."

MILES gave RACHEL a tentative hug.

"No, MILES. More hug."

"Okay Camera 2, I want you to pull back into a two shot. Camera 3, I want a take on MILES." Lavinia made a quick notation on her clipboard. "Where's JANICE?"

"I'm in the kitchen, sweetheart," a voice called from the other end of the studio. "Where else?"

Everyone laughed a little, and all the action shifted away.

"So you're Kerwin's daughter," Hugh said to me. "What a pretty girl he has. One I'm delighted to have as my new daughter."

I smiled weakly. I still hadn't forgiven Riverford's most illustrious surgeon for letting DEREK SIMMONS die.

"I never expected to have such an old child myself, that's more Kerwin's speed." Hugh winked at me while my mother happened to be looking the other way.

"I never expected to have such a distinguished surgeon as my father. I hope I do you justice."

"I'm sure you will, my dear. I'm sure."

"MILES!" Lavinia called. "MILES! You're missing your cue!"

"Gotta run," he said and trotted away.

I already knew that if I wasn't careful, he'd be trouble.

"You're going to do just fine," my mother said in a whisper.

I shrugged and waited in silence for my next scene.

We broke at 12:30 for lunch, but I had to eat standing up in front of the wardrobe mistress. Someone had goofed and decided RACHEL would wear cowboy boots since she was from Montana. With just plain boot heels, I was six feet tall, almost a foot taller than most of the other actresses. None of the shirts for the women fit me unless they were supposed to have three-quarter sleeves.

"Listen," Shirley said into the phone. "I don't care what she's supposed to wear. She looks like a giant in what I've got for her. No one told me she was six feet tall . . . well, what do you want me to do about it? . . . Mr. DeMeglio please, let's not be ridiculous. I can't run out and get her something else now . . . they're taping in three hours . . . go ahead . . ."

I took a bite of the corned beef sandwich my mother had gotten me from a nearby delicatessen. I didn't know I wasn't allowed to be this tall. My father was tall, my mother was tall, I was just following in their footsteps.

Shirley hung up the phone with a loud crack. "You'll just have to wear your streetclothes for today."

I stared at her.

"Those are the orders. Maybe in a week I'll have something for you. Unless you want to wear WOODIE's clothes . . . nothing else here is your size."

"Who's WOODIE?"

"The new kid. The District Attorney's son. Very rich."

"Oh forget it," I replied and walked out of the room.

"Gene says you're to wear flat shoes from now on. They won't shoot you full length," Shirley called, poking her head around the doorway.

"The could just shoot me sitting down all the time," I answered and walked down the hall to make-up, which was empty so I sat down in one of the barbershop type chairs.

"I'll be right with you, okay?" A woman walked in the room carrying an aluminum plate of food.

"Sure."

She ate standing up, watching a game show play on the television set perched on top of the gray lockers at the end of the room. "I'm Rhoda," she told me during a commercial break.

"I'm Kate Rafferty."

"Kerwin's daughter."

I smiled slightly.

"I was so sorry DEREK was killed off. We all were. Your father is such a nice man, we never had any trouble with him, like we do with . . . oh well," she said as she wiped a paper napkin across her lips. "Well," she said looking at me in the mirror. "I think we'll have to tone you down a bit." Rhoda picked up a triangular piece of sponge and a palette of pancake make-up in various shades. She dabbed the sponge and started to put it on my face.

"Wait a minute," I said touching her arm with my hand. "What do you mean, tone me down?" Somehow that seemed scary. Mom? Where are you when I need you?

"Your skintone is more colorful than anyone else's. When the camera picks up on it, you'll stick out."

"This is my coloring. I don't wear make-up, and I don't want to be toned down."

Her face grew hard in the mirror. I wasn't as cooperative as my father, I suppose. She shrugged. "Okay, but tell them it was all your idea."

My mother showed up when I was having my hair washed by Antonio. "I just had a nice chat with Roxanne," she said speaking of the associate producer.

"What'd she have to say?" I asked as Antonio nearly rubbed my hair off with a towel.

"She says the writers are going to come up with an entirely new story line devoted to young people, high school and college. Within the next few months the show is going to change drastically."

"I thought that's what they had already decided. It's not a news flash."

"Sure it is. This is a massive, large-scale alteration. They're going to hire about ten new people besides the ones they've already found."

"What's it got to do with me?"

"I'm just telling you what to expect. You won't just be MILES' daughter, there will be other people your age, and contemporary themes."

"Sounds fascinating," I said with no emotion.

"You can never tell, Kate," she replied, then stopped talking because Antonio was using a blow dryer on my hair.

"I'm supposed to let it be natural today. Just blow," Antonio told me as he put the dryer down and began brushing my hair with a stiff bristled brush.

"Fine," I replied. "After all, RACHEL's been on a bus for a day and a half or something. You can't expect her to come into Riverford looking like she just finished a photo session at Scavullo's."

Antonio finished, and my mother and I began to walk back to the studio. "Are you in costume. Did you red chair before you changed?"

Red chair means to have your hair done. "This is my costume for today. Looks rather slept in doesn't it?"

"Kate, you're not making your debut in jeans, a flannel shirt and boating mocassins."

"Want to bet?"

We went through the heavy gray door into the dark studio. Lavinia was standing by the table, pouring a cup of coffee. "You're supposed to be in costume, RACHEL."

"Yeah, well, talk to Shirley about that. The only clothes they have to fit me seem to belong to a guy named WOODIE."

"I thought you were supposed to send all your sizes down last week."

"We did," my mother said.

Lavinia shook her head and said nothing as she went back out the gray door to the control room.

On our way to the FERGUSON living room, we passed the FERGUSON kitchen, the bar at Ship's Rail, the second hottest eatery in town—the first being The Water's Edge Inn —and one hospital room.

"Five minutes," Lavinia called over the intercom. "MILES, are you in the studio?"

34

"Yes, Lavinia," MILES answered from his seat atop his leather-top desk.

"When you close the door after RACHEL walks in, I want you to lean slightly up against the door, as if you've just had a big shock."

"Gotcha. No problem there at all."

The studio became very quiet; people tiptoed around; no one spoke.

"Quiet on the set," Jack, the a.d., called unnecessarily.

We ran through the rehearsal, took a fifteen minute break and came back to the studio for the taping.

Everyone kept asking me if I was nervous. I wasn't. Both Gene and Lavinia had told me about fifty times that they didn't care how I sounded, just as long as I did not *look at the camera*. There's a teleprompter box attached to the front side of each camera, and when actors go up on their lines, the teleprompter is there with a continuous roll of the script. But it looks dumb to use it; there's no way to finesse reading lines off the teleprompter. Since my mother had helped me with the script, I felt pretty secure. That and the fact that my father had had me reciting since I was old enough to stand: "Ye Gods! It doth amaze me. A man of such a feeble temper should so get the start of the majestic world and bear the palm alone." I can only believe my father had me learn those lines from Shakespeare because he thought it was a very cute idea.

Now he was home honing up on his piano playing. And I couldn't help but think he was a little jealous, or maybe not jealous but feeling ignored. It's very difficult for a true ham to be at any point other than center stage. And I, on the other hand, didn't have anything to prove. My ego wasn't on the line. It was money, that was all.

"All right," Lavinia said over the intercom.

Jack began watching his stopwatch and signaled for MILES to begin.

35

I stood by the door waiting for my cue to knock and enter. I wondered if I was breathing so loud that the sound boom would pick me up.

MILES picked up the phone. I watched him in one of the many monitors hanging from the ceiling. "That's right, PAUL. I think MR. JENKINS has cerebral damage. We have to go in immediately."

Poor guy. JENKINS was a goner.

MILES gave a beat, pretending to listen to what the nonexistent person on the other end of the phone said, then replied "I can get the O.R. for ten tomorrow. We don't dare wait a minute longer. I'll get back to you." He hung up.

I knocked.

MILES came to the door and opened it.

"Dad?" I asked.

MILES stood there looking properly bewildered.

"It's me, Dad, RACHEL." My voice quivered just as we had rehearsed it.

"RACHEL, darling. What are you doing here?" MILES asked coming toward me.

"Mom died. In an automobile accident last week. I didn't have anyplace else to go. May I stay here?"

MILES took RACHEL in his arms, and as he did, the camera came in for a close-up of MILES' face, called a take, and Hugh gave me a firm squeeze on the fanny.

"Okay," Lavinia called. "Terrific, RACHEL, you're a natural. Okay, JANICE. . . ."

Hugh pulled away from me and gave me a big wink.

I was just hoping the writers weren't foreseeing a close relationship between MILES and RACHEL. I didn't want to be fighting Hugh's hands in every clinch.

Six

"Hi, I'm fonda."

I looked up into my mirror to see a dark-haired girl standing behind me.

"I've been waiting to meet you for two weeks. I wanted to get to know you since we're destined to be archrivals and at least roommates." She laughed and plunked herself down in the chair that faced the opposite mirror.

I swiveled my chair around to look at her. With thick, deep brown hair and pale skin, she had a fragile, delicate look.

"My real name's Ellin. I'm from New York and I just got off a six month run on BETWEEN OUR LIVES."

"Hi."

"I've been hearing about you ever since I got this job."

"Did they kill you?"

"On LIVES you mean? No." She pulled a brush from her duffle bag and began running it through her hair. "The tangles I get, but I sell better with long hair than short. Then I look like a pixie. It was a six month character, a drippy cousin who went off to nursing school. Now I'll be a rich, spoiled brat."

"They made a good choice. You look very . . ."

"You can say it. I love to play a good witchy character, a schemer, totally self-centered. The last part was such a wimp."

"I think RACHEL is pretty bland myself."

"Have you worked before?"

"No. My father used to be DEREK SIMMONS, but he's

37

back to being Kerwin Rafferty now."

"How old are you?"

"Just turned seventeen in August."

"A Leo."

I nodded.

"I'm twenty. I spent a year and a half in the drama department at Carnegie-Mellon and then decided to start working seriously. I've done a couple of commercials but this is going to be my biggest part. FONDA was resurrected from a Swiss boarding school, and she's the daughter of a Spanish count. What does that make me? A countette?"

I had to laugh along with her.

"I think we'll be good friends. In LIVES I shared my dressing room with the most impossible female in the world. Want to go to lunch together?"

"Sure. You mean eat out?"

"Of course. Have you been eating here every day? Alone?"

I nodded.

"I get it. The family hasn't accepted you yet."

"You could say that."

Ellin flipped her hair back and tied it with a ribbon. "They can sense a change coming, and they want to test the water before they jump in. The whole show is going to be turned upside down, you wait and see. It's that or get cancelled. In a real blood bath like this, no one knows who'll get the axe next. You don't know how jealous these people can get."

"I know, my father's in the business."

She stood. I closed my book, and we left for the studio. Lavinia made her five minute call for breakdown over the intercom.

"They're hiring some of the most outrageous people," Ellin told me as we walked into the studio. "Where's LOUISE's living room today?" she asked Jack, who pointed to the end of the room. "Good. We can talk in peace. So RACHEL and JANICE pay a call on LOUISE and FONDA this afternoon, for a spot of tea. Knowing FONDA, she'll put horseradish in the teapot."

We passed technical people, grips, electricians, finishing up the sets. FRED HEGARTY was in PAUL's office, preparing for his medical checkup, promising to have dire results.

"What do you mean outrageous?"

"Some of the people have no experience. *None.*"

"I have no experience, *none,* unless of course you want to count my one-night run as a defoliating dahlia."

"But your father's in the business. You're not really a civilian like some of these people. Wait till you meet WOODIE."

We sat on a couch and even under the bright lights it was cold.

"I keep hearing about this WOODIE. Who is he, and when does he show up?"

"Peter, Petah Searle," she said with an upper crust accent. "It's a case of nepotism. His mom is the cousin of someone blah-blah. He acted in high school. I mean, can you imagine. I had to do the test with him. He can't act at all. Ellin, stop being so catty!" she remonstrated, with herself, then laughed. "He's going to be your boyfriend," Ellin whispered as she leaned over to me.

"WHAT?" I said too loudly. "What?"

"RACHEL's boyfriend anyway, you just wait and see. I'll bet that's what happens. The REYDEL's are a rich family —the father is the local D.A.—and WOODIE is a good catch for anyone."

"Then why would he be interested in RACHEL."

"So FONDA and RACHEL can have something to fight over."

"You can have him. I won't fight over a guy."

"You'll see. Hi ya, Mummie," Ellin called as LOUISE, Marilyn Grimes, walked onto the set.

"Why don't you go back to Spain and live with your ne'er-do-well father?" Marilyn replied. "My life isn't my own since you came back to Riverford."

That had been in yesterday's script, when LOUISE had been in a drunken stupor. It wasn't one of my days, so I hadn't been there to see it.

"But, Mummie. Don't you love your one and only daughter, cherished FONDA?"

"No! Hi, Kathleen. I'm glad to meet you. Been hearing about you, but our days haven't met. Your father and I had such good times together. Do you know we had an affair about six months ago?"

I looked at her blankly for a moment. Then it registered. "Right. LOUISE and DEREK."

"Why, of course," Marilyn smiled. "We're all happily married here, aren't we, Mir?"

Miriam Stern stepped carefully over two sets of thick black cables and looked up. "All my husbands were wonderful men."

"Mir . . ."

"Except Stuart, now he was very difficult to take. And of course there was Bob, he was very jealous. And Ron . . . well, Ron is another thing all together. But you should meet Howard. He's a prince among men."

"Or a frog among princes?" Marilyn asked, and we all laughed.

"Howard's on the news desk across town," Miriam told me. "Not network, local, but moving up fast. They brought him in . . ."

"From Philly. Can you believe it?" Marilyn supplied.

"Someone has to come from Philadelphia, and you can say what you like," Miriam said as she tucked her blouse tighter into her skirt. "But he's in the business. It took me three marriages to realize civilians don't understand what we go through. If I can give you kids any advice, it's to marry someone in the industry."

"These are real marriages then?" I asked.

Marilyn threw back her head and laughed heartily. "I don't know how real they were, do you, Mir?"

"That's a question I've asked myself, but yes, Kathleen, these were marriages in real life. I've only been married twice on the show, but if MILES doesn't quit fooling around with DANIELLE, I might just leave him and start looking for someone new."

Jack came over with two cameras and a boom. Lavinia ran through the breakdown. We didn't actually act, we just said our lines and found our marks and knew what we had to do later.

MILES gave me a wicked wink across the studio from his set, a hospital office. I half smiled back at him. I didn't want to encourage him, but I didn't want to alienate him either. He was going to be my father for the next ten weeks, and if everything went really well, for six months after that. But if everything went that well, someone might shoot him. Maybe MRS. JENKINS.

We broke for lunch; Ellin and I rushed into our coats and zipped out of the building before anyone could delay us. With only an hour to eat, we didn't have time to waste. There was a delicatessen a block away from the studio that catered to that network and all the people in the industry, and we were lucky enough to get a table in the back. As we waited for our order to be served, Ellin sat back and studied me carefully.

"I'm surprised they hired two dark-haired females to play against each other. You should have been a blonde. Blondes don't play evil parts, not often anyway. Why are you working now?"

"Um . . ." I didn't think it was such a good idea to let it out into the open that the Raffertys needed money.

"You've studied to be an actress?"

"No."

"You got the job because you knew the right people."

"I suppose that's as good a reason as any. It just all happened. One day I was in high school, and the next I was signed for thirteen weeks. I still haven't figured it out."

"You be careful, Kate. Listen to what I tell you, this business can eat you up alive. And you never know what the future's going to bring. I haven't been in it long, but with the way the ratings are dropping, something spectacular has to happen fast or we'll all be out of work."

"I keep hearing that stuff, but I haven't seen much action."

"Haven't you been reading all the scripts?"

"Not really, they're a real bore."

She smiled. "You'd better start. They're bringing in a lot of new people, competition, girl. Best be prepared."

"I'm just a background character. I'm not in competition for anything: more lines, more close-ups, a bigger dressing room. Nothing."

She shrugged. "Let's see if you can say that after we've had ALISON around for a while. She's WOODIE's stepsister, and this girl is on her way to superstardom; her agent says so. This is just a stepping-stone on her road to the glittering lights of Hollywood."

The waiter brought the sandwiches, and Ellin looked at me thoughtfully. "I think you've got some surprises coming. Some of these people are going to provide a real adventure."

"So who or what is so fascinating, so surprising?"

"Have you met CAREY CROSS, WOODIE's poverty-stricken cousin?"

"Met him? I haven't even heard of him."

"Oh Kate, he's worked three days already. CAREY's being played by a native Californian named Fitch Cooper."

"Is that his real name?"

"Yes. A family name. I asked. We're playing a scene together tomorrow, and it'd be worth it for you to come watch."

I shook my head as I swallowed. "Nothing is so important that I'd drive over a hundred and fifty miles when I wasn't working."

Ellin laughed. "When you see CAREY CROSS you won't say that."

Seven

"How's it going down there?"

I pulled on my sheepskin coat and grabbed my duffle bag. "Fine, Dad."

Still sleepy and groggy, in his bathrobe, he sat down on the front stairs. "You're getting along with Lavinia? She can be a bulldozer sometimes. No one's giving you any trouble?"

"No. Everything is fine; but it's already eight, and I'm going to be late."

"You had a late call then."

"Yeah."

"How many pages did you have to learn today?"

"Eleven."

He nodded. "Be careful when you drive home. The roads might be slippery. Maybe when your contract comes up for renegotiation, we'll get you a limo."

I opened the front door. "Absolutely not."

He shrugged.

I closed the door and rushed to my Jeep, either a late or a very early birthday present, but actually more of a necessity to insure my getting to work no matter how horrendous the weather became this winter. I didn't need a limo; I didn't want a limo, and I wouldn't get it even if I asked for one. I wasn't even a secondary player on the show; tertiary maybe, but I'd get no concessions.

My father was still moping around the house. Everything was going against him, he said. Summer package show casting was months away, and the dinner theater route was all set for the season. He said this was the winter of his discontent. And I guess it was.

The Jeep bounced along the backroads, sending clouds of fine snowdust into the air behind me. Even if we didn't finish taping until seven, I wasn't worried about getting home. I'd just throw my trusty Jeep into four-wheel drive and buzz along.

Driving in alone gave me time to think. Since I had gotten the Jeep, my mother had stopped babysitting with me. Everything was going well, and she could see that she'd be of more use staying home holding Dad's hand. The Jeep wasn't as comfortable as the Mercedes anyway.

RACHEL was going to Riverford High now. FONDA thought of her as a goody-two-shoes and never passed up an opportunity to say so. WOODIE REYDEL had sat with RACHEL in the luncheonette several times, and that had left FONDA fuming.

I was surprised at how much venom Ellin could summon as FONDA, and it made me feel that RACHEL was extremely one-dimensional, a character who never lost her temper, who never vented any emotions, who just proceeded from scene to scene in an almost zombie-like abstraction. I was playing RACHEL the way it was written and the way Lavinia directed, and I didn't like it at all. But I wasn't being paid to like RACHEL.

Marcia came over every weekend to tell me how wonderfully I was doing. And she wanted to know all about CAREY CROSS.

Almost every time I turned around, I was hearing about this CAREY CROSS, but we still hadn't been on a show together. If I worked three days one week, CAREY CROSS worked two. If I worked two, he worked three but not four. And I hadn't caught him on the tube, so I knew nothing of what everyone seemed to be getting so agitated over.

As Ellin had suggested, I had been reading all the scripts,

not just those I appeared in. I knew something about CAREY CROSS, but it was even less than Marcia had learned.

CAREY CROSS was WOODIE REYDEL's cousin, a branch of the wealthy REYDEL family that had not done particularly well. CAREY was attending Riverford College and seemed to have a huge chip on his shoulder. WOODIE bothered him, which didn't surprise me since WOODIE also bothered me. And Ellin said CAREY would wind up as the male counterpart of FONDA, very evil, Riverford's new resident bad boy. I didn't know why she always seemed to know how the story lines would turn before anyone else, but she did.

I passed the Stella D'Oro Bakery along the Major Deegan Freeway and got a whiff of all those delicious smells. At least it was still there. The Wechsler Coffee plant that used to roast beans further along—which had smelled much better than a plain cup of coffee—had closed down.

Today was the big day. Today was the day I was going to meet up with CAREY CROSS, in the luncheonette where everyone hung out. Eateries are big business in serials.

I had called Marcia when I received the script to tell her this would be the day she had been waiting for. Tomorrow I could tell her what CAREY CROSS was like in real life.

I suppose she had a crush on him or something.

I parked the car in the garage closest to the studio and walked the half block to the entrance. The security guard waved me through, and I went directly to my dressing room where Ellin was eating a danish before the breakdown.

"I was wondering if you'd ever get here," she told me.

"I'd get here, no matter what."

"This is going to be a real experience for you."

"Meeting CAREY CROSS you mean?" I asked as I hung up my coat.

"You bet. I just have a feeling about it."

"If you're so witchy, I don't know why you can't tell me what to expect."

"Breakdown," Jack paged over the intercom.

Ellin wrapped half the danish in the thin piece of waxed paper and grabbed my arm. "Come on, I can hardly wait a minute longer." She scooted me down the long hall, and we made the turn into the studio.

My first scene was in the luncheonette, where I had been left yesterday sitting with WOODIE and his stepsister, ALISON. Because it was a rather large set, it was stuck down at the far end of the studio, taking the place of two separate sets. We made a right turn, and I could see the brightly lit luncheonette at the end of the dark studio.

"This better be good," I whispered to Ellin.

"Oh, it will be," she replied.

"Hi, RACHEL," WOODIE said.

"Hi," I said as I sat down next to him.

"The snow didn't stop you from getting here," WOODIE remarked.

"Not likely." After all, this was the big day. With Marcia so crazy about CAREY CROSS, I had to be there to report back all details about the Reydel's black-sheep relative.

ALISON joined us. Then some extras.

A shadow moved through the dark beyond the set lights. He stepped into the luncheonette. And that was my first sight of CAREY CROSS.

I just stared as he walked over to the green booth.

"If it isn't our resident sparrow, RACHEL." He held out his hand for me to shake. "I've been waiting for this meeting."

Suddenly my stomach had more knots in it than there were in a Boy Scout manual. "Why?"

His greenish eyes picked up glints from the key lights as he smiled. His hair was blond; but more than just blond, it was a combination of darker tones stuck by lighter ones, like eighteen-carat gold in the sunlight.

I guess I'd never seen anyone as attractive in my life. I wouldn't have said he was pretty; when I think of a pretty

47

guy, I think of Tyrone Power in *In Old Chicago*. I just kept thinking that this was Melville's Billy Budd. My mother would have said it was his bone structure, the fine clean lines; good bones are very important to my mother. My father would have said he was just a good-looking guy.

I didn't know what to think. I just stared, more than a little amazed, wondering how this person had wound up on this set in this show. I didn't know how it could have happened.

"Places, please," Jack said, and everyone began to move away.

CAREY CROSS went behind the set, and so did ALISON. She had been with us yesterday, but by today she had just gone.

"Okay, WOODIE," Lavinia said.

"ALISON is getting too involved with my cousin," WOODIE told me. "I've never trusted CAREY. He's out for himself, but I can't say anything to ALISON. She's just my stepsister, and I think she resents her mother's marriage to my father. She had to leave her home in Palm Beach to come here."

He was tall, too. Taller than me.

"RACHEL. It's your line," Lavinia told me.

"Uh . . ." I said. "Um . . . I'm up, what's my line?"

"ALISON's old enough to take care of herself . . ." Jack read to me off the script.

I nodded. "ALLISON's old enough to take care of herself, and if you try to interfere you might just make matters more difficult. Perhaps she'll work it out for herself."

"ALISON's had a very sheltered life so far. MARGO has treated her like a child; even now with ALISON in college, MARGO won't let go."

"Then maybe MARGO will stop the relationship before it goes too far," I replied.

"Once CAREY gets his hooks into something, he doesn't

48

give us easily. He doesn't give up at all," WOODIE said.

Those eyes were the color of Thompson seedless grapes.

"RACHEL . . ." Lavinia prompted.

I went blank again. "I'm up. What's my line?"

"What's with you today? Didn't you look at the script?" Lavinia asked.

My father had once told me about going up. Your mind repeats anything to you, frantically, furtively, replaying scenes from the last show, from your childhood, from a television commercial, anything just so there is something there. At that moment, there were two words in the entire language I knew. Carey and Cross.

"What does CAREY want with ALISON? I mean, why are you so worried, WOODIE?" Jack supplied.

"Thank you. What does CAREY want with ALISON. I mean, why are you so worried, WOODIE?" I said. Damn.

The luncheonette door opened, and CAREY CROSS fairly swaggered in. It was with an air of arrogance and supreme confidence that he crossed the set and eased himself next to me, so close our shoulders touched.

"Hi, cousin. Who's your girl friend?" CAREY asked as camera 2 came over WOODIE's shoulder for a close-up of his foxlike smile.

"RACHEL FERGUSON," WOODIE replied.

CAREY rested his hand casually on RACHEL's. "Why haven't I seen you before?"

"I'm from White Sulphur Springs, Montana. I just came to town," I replied and heard Lavinia breath an audible sigh of relief that I could manage to get one line out without prompting.

"A country girl," CAREY said. "You must know a lot about nature."

RACHEL lowered her eyes to avert CAREY's gaze, and thanks to the writers, I had time to remember my next line. "I know all I need to know."

49

"I bet we'd all be surprised at what you know," CAREY replied suggestively.

"Listen, CAREY, what do you want here?" WOODIE asked. "This is a private . . . huh?" WOODIE stopped. His eyes took on the expression of a mannequin in Bloomingdale's window.

"CONVERSATION!" Lavinia practically bellowed at him.

"Yeah, right, conversation, and we'd prefer to be alone."

"I'm sure you would. But do you know what to do with your privacy? Don't leave! As it happens, cousin, I'm looking for ALISON. We're going to have our own private conversation, though I doubt if it'll end at that," CAREY said as he stood.

ALISON walked through the door on cue, and the action moved to another booth.

I sat there and watched him work. Even though it was just the breakdown and that could never be considered acting, there was an ease, I guess grace is a better word, he possessed. It was totally obvious that he was comfortable in what he was doing.

My father had said that there are many people who can act. Some are technicians. They have a craft, and they may be very skilled but they learn by rote. No matter how good they are, there is a mechanical quality to their work. There are others who take that skill and add something of themselves to it. When it comes together, it's magic. It's as if some people have a well full of all kinds of emotions and attitudes and mannerisms that they can touch and mold and bend whenever they need them. Other people are like the desert and need to have an outside source fill their gaps; but it's like the desert when it rains. The water just drains away leaving sand.

Now I knew what my father meant.

Before I realized it, the scene was over, and Lavinia and

her rolling podium moved into the further recesses of the studio.

CAREY came over to me and put his hand on my shoulder. "What say we have lunch together."

". . . Sure."

"I'll meet you in the lobby."

"Okay."

He walked away for his next scene with ALISON.

Eight

WE WALKED THE THREE BLOCKS to the restaurant, and he held
open the massive bolted oak door for me. Inside it was so
dark, I could barely see, and if it weren't for the maitre d'
dressed in monk's robes, I probably would have fallen right
down the stairs leading to the dining room.

I had already decided to order the easiest thing to eat;
I didn't want to choke on food, so I ordered a bowl of soup.
Then I realized that with my sophistication, the soup would
probably drip on my chin.

"Hi," he said to me as the waiter left our table with the
orders.

"Hi."

"What do your friends call you?"

"Kate, just Kate. Kathleen is someone else."

"Okay, Just-Kate. So you're new to this then."

"Yes. Is it that obvious?"

He smiled, but it wasn't that CAREY CROSS expression.
And it wasn't a CAREY CROSS' voice; there was a completely different quality to it, softer, smoother, missing that
knife-like edge. "No. It just takes a while before you get
used to being called by your character name or by your professional name. Your father's Kerwin Rafferty, isn't he?"

I nodded.

"He's a fine actor. I was fascinated by his portrayal of
DEREK SIMMONS. At one time LIFE was up against the
show I was on, so I'd catch the competition when I could, but
that was several years ago. After I was hired for LIFE, I
tuned in, and once I saw you, I was intrigued."

"Why?"

He broke a breadstick and handed me half. "I still don't know."

"What do your friends call you?"

"Fitch."

The waiter delivered my soup and his sandwich. I felt as if I had been on a carousel too long; the center was our table and the rest was spinning out somewhere else, just a blur. I knew I should talk, but I had nothing to say. "Been in the business long?"

"Since I was four. I've done commercials, voice-overs, a couple of cartoons. I did Buddy Lewis, boy space pilot."

"That cartoon that's been on for years?"

"Think of the residuals. In some markets it plays twice a day. I've done some film work, some prime time, and a couple of soaps on the coast. I keep busy. What have you done?"

"Nothing. This is it, unless you count a disaster in grade school. Maybe you're reading me older than I am. I'm seventeen."

"You do read older. But then so do I. Maybe that's because I've been in the industry for so long. All I ever wanted to do was act."

"That's what my father says. He's been searching his whole life for an audience."

He must have thought I was at least as old as Ellin. He seemed so much older than I felt. Too tall and awkward and unable to carry on an intelligent conversation, I felt something like a fish made of ice I had once seen decorate a buffet table. "Where'd you get a name like Fitch?"

"It's a family name, my mother's maiden name."

Even in the low light, his hair caught the illumination and took on a soft sheen. "You know, you're even prettier than people tell me I am."

Leaning back in his chair, he laughed so hard tears came to his eyes. And I almost died of embarrassment. Some day, I had vowed, I would learn what not to say. Except I never knew what I was going to say until it was too late.

He wiped his eyes and took a deep breath. "That's just what I said about you the first time I caught the show."

I didn't reply because I really didn't know what he meant.

"I think you and I have a lot in common," he said handing the waiter his credit card. "One of which is that we're going to be late."

Glancing at my watch, I saw it was almost one-thirty. Lavinia would have a conniption if we were late for dress rehearsal. It was such an unprofessional thing to do, to be late; we ran back to the studio, literally ran, and arrived in time absolutely out of breath. It was great. For the first time in weeks, I felt unchic, unsophisticated and totally myself.

As I dashed past my dressing room, Ellin caught up with me and handed me a pink envelope.

"What's this?" I asked as we went into the studio. Luckily I had changed before lunch.

"They sent it from upstairs. Maybe it's your first fan letter."

"Sure."

We split up at the center of the studio; she went to LOUISE's living room, and I went to the luncheonette. I still had time before my scene so I opened the letter.

Dear RACHEL,

I have been watching LIFE TO ITS FULLEST for years but it's never been so interesting as it is now that you're on. I hope MILES treats you well, but with this trouble in his marriage to JANICE, you might be in for a rough time. He's having an affair with DANIELLE, and she's pushing him to get a divorce and marry her. I know you've had it hard enough in your life, losing your mother and all, so I figured you should be prepared for the worst. Also, do not under any circumstances trust CAREY CROSS. He hates his cousin WOODIE, and I know how much you like WOODIE and WOODIE likes you, so CAREY would like to destroy that relationship. Since you two are a perfect pair and CAREY is so evil, he's set out to make WOODIE miserable in whatever way he can. CAREY is into some very underhanded and probably illegal doings; anyone who comes in contact with him should be careful. Please listen to my advice before anything bad happens.

Your friend,
Betty

My first fan letter. From an absolute cashew.

I wasn't RACHEL. I was Kate. And I wondered why Betty couldn't see the difference.

My father had gotten his share of fan mail, and sometimes people even sent him gifts—little books of poetry or a handknitted scarf at Christmas—but I had never thought about getting anything myself. It was just something that happened to him and had nothing to do with me. But this Betty was happening to me, and I began to wonder if I was going to start getting fan mail from then on. Getting mail wasn't really all good. Not when I sort of had a responsibility to reply to Betty.

Dear Betty,

Thank you very much for your letter and expression of concern, but your fears are groundless. I am running away with CAREY CROSS tomorrow. We are getting married in Reno, Nevada, and will run a con operation in Las Vegas.

Sincerely,
RACHEL FERGUSON CROSS

No, that wouldn't work at all. Maybe I could persuade Marcia to answer my fan mail for me. Maybe she'd do it for a fee and a promise to meet CAREY CROSS in absolute *real life*.

Was RACHEL going to get involved with CAREY? Marcia always asked me if that's where we were going, but I didn't know; she hoped we would because we'd look so good together.

That's all I needed. What would it be like to play a lot of scenes with Fitch. I could see myself perpetually going up on my lines, perpetually tongue-tied and eventually looking as dumb as WOODIE. I was starting to feel inadequate. It had never mattered much to me that I hadn't acted before; I didn't care if I did really well or not, all I wanted was to last nine months and get the money for my father. But if I was going to have to play against Fitch, he would know I didn't have the slightest idea of what I was doing. Somehow I had been getting by and not looking too much like an amateur, but I knew I couldn't measure up to someone really good.

At any other time in his life, my father would have been glad to help me. But now was not the right time to ask him to be my dramatic coach. It would be too depressing for him to think he had been relegated to a position behind the cameras.

My life was starting to get too complicated. I had never wanted to become this involved in LIFE. I didn't want to be an actress. I didn't want to be in show business.

I folded the letter into a tight square and slipped it into my pocket, then closed my eyes. It was so quiet for a moment that it all seemed to go away. If it was possible anywhere to close my eyes and make everything go back to normal, it ought to be possible here in fantasyland.

"Places, please," Jack called.

WOODIE came over and sat across from me.

Fitch crossed the set going toward the luncheonette door and winked at me.

For a moment, I was sure I had imagined it. He wouldn't wink at me.

I remember the story my Grandmother Rafferty had told me about the days when she was an actress in Hollywood. She had been playing a bit part in "Stagecoach," and there was a stunt man playing one of the cowboys. She said he was so good looking, it just made her heart go all a-twitter. No matter how many times I had heard that story, it still made me laugh when she said that word.

That cowboy was my Grandfather Rafferty.

I wasn't laughing now.

Nine

I WAS GETTING CONFUSED. Things were happening too fast. After the first scene I played with Fitch, the fan mail started to pour in. Green envelopes, white, flowered, scented, everything the post office would allow.

Marcia said this was in response to the chemistry we had on the tube. She kept asking what he was like in real life, as if I wasn't tellng her everything, as if I was hiding something from her. But then, everyone wanted to know what he was like. My father wanted to know. My mother wanted to know. But they wanted to know what he was like in regard to me. Was he a nice boy, not a dirty young lech, etc.? They didn't ask that exactly, but I knew it was on my mother's mind. ("She's just seventeen, Kerwin, a baby.")

Everyone else wanted to know how RACHEL could stand to be in the same room with CAREY CROSS, as if he radiated evil vibes strong enough to strike someone dead at ten paces. CAREY CROSS was the most evil dude on television. He was heavy into selling dope on the college campus and had even begun to get ALISON hooked on the stuff. He had underworld connections. (Betty, how did you know?) He used women as playthings. He had no regard or respect for his poor mother or his ailing grandmother. He betrayed the only friend he had. CAREY CROSS was well and truly terrible. He fascinated the audience, repelled them, and they loved it.

I had no trouble differentiating between the two. CAREY CROSS was fiction. Fitch was real, and because of his talent, could make people believe there was a CAREY CROSS.

Fitch never walked past the carriage horses lined up next to Central Park without remarking that it should be illegal for the horses to eat off the filthy street and stand all day in the cold. If he passed a street vendor, he'd bring a flower to place in my hair. None of that was CAREY.

Watching Fitch perform never ceased to enthrall me because I continually learned from him. Some people can't handle a prop. Some people can't stand in one spot and look comfortable. Some people can't finesse their way around another actor who makes a mistake. By watching Fitch, I could see how these things could be done. I couldn't do it, but he could. There was technique. I saw how a complete character is built from the ground up, layer upon layer, until it was no surprise to me that everyone believed CAREY was the devil incarnate. Fitch was damn good at what he did. And the further a character is from the real person, the more obvious the actor's talent becomes.

I wasn't spending much time with "the family" these days, not even FONDA; preferring to stay with Fitch, just reading or talking about nothing much in particular. Yet sometimes I'd catch a quick glance, an eye-take or just a change in posture that made me feel Fitch wasn't being accepted. I told my father that CAREY CROSS was such an evil character and Fitch was so talented that he had everyone in Riverford, even in real life, believing he was this terrible person. My father said that would be unprofessional. But I wasn't convinced that "the family" was above being unprofessional if they felt threatened.

We closed up shop early on a Friday in mid-December because of a snowstorm, and I drove home, the flakes swirling in front of my headlights. It was a long trip, but I didn't notice the time. I just kept thinking about the scenes I had done.

CAREY CROSS had touched RACHEL's arm. Meaningfully. Everyone knew CAREY had his sights set on RACHEL by now. Everyone but RACHEL, of course. This was just the beginning. I couldn't help but wonder where it was all going.

As soon as I got home, I ate dinner and decided to walk to Marcia's, to sit around and talk for a while, maybe catch Merv Griffin on the tube and then walk home. My mother said I was crazy to go stomping through the fields in the middle of a snowstorm when I could just as easily call.

But I had to be alone to try to sort things out.

I didn't know what I had to figure out. Every time I started to think about Fitch and me, I brought myself up short. I would allow myself to think about him, but not about us. My problem was that I was afraid of making more of whatever lay between us than actually was there. Having come from a different part of the country, and with practically the whole "family" ignoring him, he didn't have anyone to turn to but me. Given half a chance, anyone could see that Fitch was nothing like CAREY, and "the family" was having a collective anxiety attack for nothing.

Well, maybe that wasn't quite true. I was beginning to understand some of the things my father had told me one day while he was sanding the back stairs and speaking about the craft of acting.

Everyone carries inside the possibility for every human emotion available. Some people are naturally more aggressive or gregarious or vulnerable or hostile or countless things, but everyone has everything. My father said that acting involves looking inside for an experience that triggers a response, even a small one. Then the actor takes that emotion and builds on it.

Fitch was very eloquent; he brought a smoothness to the character of CAREY CROSS that made the part seem more evil than even Dave Dietz had imagined. When someone extremely good looking also managed to appear extremely sinister, the result was instant distrust. My father quoted the poet, Rainer Maria Rilke, when he spoke about Fitch. "Beauty is but the first degree of the terrible." CAREY CROSS had gone beyond the first degree.

In the past two weeks, my father had taken to watching the show and seemed to understand CAREY CROSS perfectly, but then he had been Riverford's resident bad boy prior to Fitch's arrival. When I told him RACHEL seemed incredibly bland, he said that was because I was bringing nothing of myself to her. But I didn't know how to remedy that. I was just grateful he found my work adequate.

Brushing snow off a stone wall, I sat down. I could hear the snow falling around me.

If CAREY CROSS made a move on RACHEL, I knew I was going to be uncomfortable. Fitch and I were friends; I couldn't really imagine our relationship being more than that. But still, I was being a jerk. Somewhere in my social development I must have missed a crush I was scheduled to have, and this was it. Late and behind and inconvenient. I guess I knew I could never be just Fitch's buddy. But that was what he wanted, I was sure; so that's all what we had together was or could be. I knew that, but it didn't stop me from being dumb anyway.

When I was with him, I got all confused.

"I don't understand anything." I said it aloud and the words came back, dulled by the heavy snow. "It's all Sylvia's fault." I stood. "It's all MILES FERGUSON's fault. He's just a quack doctor. Why doesn't the AMA take his license away?"

I stomped my way across the field to the Loesch house.

Marcia came to the door after I knocked. "You're covered with snow."

"I guess that's possible."

"Do you want some cocoa?" she asked as I followed her into the kitchen. "I saw the show today. It was so good. When CAREY kissed ALISON, I just about thought I'd die. He's so sexy. Is he that sexy in real life? When does CAREY make a play for RACHEL? You're so lucky."

"I don't know anything about it, and I didn't see the show. Marcia, please . . ."

"You two are perfect together. Forget that drip WOODIE and concentrate on CAREY. Everyone at school is dying for you to get together. They adore CAREY, of course he is just so rotten . . . What are you so gloomy about?"

"The girls like Fitch?"

"Are you kidding me! He's so cute."

That didn't make me feel any better.

"Did you see the new issue of *Daystars?*"

I shook my head. Magazines. What did I need with them?

"Just wait," she said as she ran out of the kitchen. In a minute, she was back and placed an open magazine in front of me.

There I was. My photo.

"Read it."

" 'Kathleen Rafferty, newcomer playing RACHEL FER-GUSON on LTIF, is receiving a great deal of attention from the viewers. She's sure to go far in her chosen field. Acting runs in the family; father Kerwin was ex-DEREK SIMMONS on LTIF. We wish her much success.' "

"Isn't that fabulous?" Marcia was so enthusiastic, I felt more like bland ol' RACHEL than ever before.

"Big deal."

"Big deal? You're going to be a star and look," she thumbed through the pages, "you made the Top Ten!"

"The Top Ten what?"

"Favorite actresses. You made it without being on the list

first. You're number nine. It's incredible! You're going to be a big star."

Oh yeah. That was really important. That was what we were all in the business for. To get a *name*. To become a *star*. The bigger the better. I didn't care how much "ensemble" talk "the family" threw around, every time DANIELLE got some publicity (she had been number two on the list for forty-three issues), being famous mattered to them.

"Here's ALISON," I pointed out. "She came in at number eight."

"Deanna Davison doesn't count. She was on the list from her part of LOVE EVER AFTER."

I shrugged. "I don't belong in this business. I'm a fake. I don't know what I'm doing.'

"It's instinctive. Don't be silly, you're every bit as good as anyone else on the show."

I might have been as good as WOODIE, but I couldn't be compared to Fitch, who was a real professional. He could sense where the camera was, and gave the most incredibly subtle reactions and inflections. He could control a scene. I'd seen him do it with WOODIE; Fitch could manipulate Pete without Pete's even knowing it. Fitch knew exactly what he was doing at all times.

"You've got a real future in this business. If you could only see yourself objectively. Listen, Kate, maybe things are just happening too fast and you need a while to get used to it."

I nodded. Maybe that was it. I felt as if I was being inundated. I had never been a letter writer, and now each week, there were grocery bags full of mail from people who expected me to write back. "Marcia, will you handle my fan mail for me? Be my secretary?" I didn't have the strength to tackle all those letters, presents, broken and smashed cookies, the scarves and mittens.

"Really? You're serious? You're not kidding?"

"It's not like I'm doing you a favor, Marcia. You don't know . . ."

"Oh wow. I'd love to do it! I can't believe it. Oh thank you."

I shrugged. Now I was becoming a business. Kate Rafferty, Inc. I beg your pardon. Kathleen Rafferty. And secretary.

The phone rang, and Mrs. Loesch picked it up on the living room. "Kate, it's for you!"

I picked up the receiver from the wall phone. "Hello?"

"Kate! Sylvia just called with the most fantastic news!" My mother was breathless.

"What." I was instantly suspicious. Sylvia was out to get me. She wanted me to be a Big Star.

"You've got a luncheon appointment at Cafe Des Aristes on Monday with *View* Magazine. They want to do an article on you!"

Yea.

"Kate?"

"I'm here."

"Isn't that wonderful?"

"Wonderful."

"Are you coming home soon. We have to make plans for this interview. It'll be so important to your career."

"I'll be home soon. Bye." I hung up. I didn't want to be interviewed. I just wanted to put in my time, have a car accident and get a ruptured spleen or something and die before MILES could perform one of his miraculous splenectomies on me.

Ten

I CHANGED IN MY DRESSING ROOM and glanced toward the wall clock. It was going to be a quick lunch-slash-interview combination since I had only an hour before I had to get back, change for dress and do make-up.

"Going?"

Fitch was waiting for me in the hall. I nodded.

"Great dress."

It was a very old-fashioned style, what the Victorians called a day dress, that I had made in dark blue and burgundy calicos and had shortened from its standard full length because I wouldn't schlep around Manhattan in a full length anything. I wasn't as crazy about clothes as my mother, but I had learned to sew from her as she had from her mother, and if we ever thought I needed something, we'd whip it up. Buying things off the rack seemed like a waste of money, especially when we'd have to alter it anyway. "Thanks. My mother says I should have used a lighter color with the blue because it's too dark."

"You made it?" he asked in amazement.

"Well, sure. You can't find this in a store." People always seemed so surprised to hear that we made most of our clothes, but it was normal for us.

We started toward the door.

"You should wear that dress on the show."

"RACHEL wouldn't wear something like this. She wears Peter Pan collars and clothes straight out of the early Sixties."

"You could start to change RACHEL by beginning with the little things. Let her grow and learn how to use your muscles, Kate. You're going to be big."

I stopped in the hall and looked at him, as if he had given me a seal of approval.

"Does that surprise you? It shouldn't."

I shrugged. It all depended on what you called big. Was I going to be a professional, or was I going to turn out to be a Faith Hunter, a non-talent? "My father used to tell me there were four stages to this profession all depending on casting directors. The first stage is Who's Kerwin Rafferty. The second is Get me Kerwin Rafferty. The third is Get me a Kerwin Rafferty type. The fourth is Who's Kerwin Rafferty."

Fitch smiled. "You'd better be prepared because you're coming into the Get me Kate Rafferty stage. But just let me give you a little advice from someone who's been working for a pretty long time. If you act as though you don't care what they do with you, you'll have treadprints from their running shoes all over your face."

"I just want RACHEL to go away to have an abortion or something in six months."

"That's not really likely. There's a lot of talk going around the network that all this emphasis on the youth market has attracted a new audience. What you have to realize is that when they think they've got something secure, they'll stay with it. They've raised the concept of Don't-Rock-the-Boat to a religion. If you're going out to an interview, that means people are interested. That's important."

"Not to me."

He held the door open for me, and I walked out onto the street. "But it may be very important to the network and Gene. Think about it."

I thought about it all the way to the restaurant. If RACHEL was going to be elevated to center stage, then

66

Kathleen Rafferty was going to be something of a star. No, that sounded ridiculous to me. A featured player?

No. I didn't want that either. I wanted to be in the background, anonymous. It wasn't fair to me, and it wasn't fair to my father. He had been working his whole life to be a star, and I was getting his lucky break. I didn't even want it; if I could have given it back, I would have.

I told myself not to panic as I entered the restaurant. Maybe Fitch didn't know what he was talking about. Maybe Marcia didn't know. Maybe Betty didn't know.

The woman writer waved me over to her table, and I sat down as she held out her hand. "I'm Rita Malchiodi."

"Hi. I'm Kate Rafferty."

"I'm so glad you were able to make this interview on such short notice, and I know you're short for time so what would you like to order?"

"Chicken on pumpernickel," I told the waiter.

"Chef's salad," Rita told him as she closed the menu and handed it to him. "Are you familiar with *View* Magazine?"

"Not really."

"I'm sure you're very busy finishing school and working. We like to keep our eyes open for the promising newcomers, the people with potential, the people moving upward. We like to catch trends and tell our readers what's coming up next on the horizon."

My stomach felt the same way it had when my first Dahlia petal fell off: a hesitant suggestion that something was definitely wrong. Goodbye nonchalance. Hello disaster. Ninety percent of the cast would have given their capped teeth for someone to tell them they were what was coming up next on the horizon, even if it was only in *View's* opinion.

With this interview and the blurbs in the magazines, I felt as if I were being swept away. I had a couple of hundred letters floating around in the back of my Jeep all addressed to RACHEL FERGUSON. People actually believed I was RACHEL. And those who didn't think I was RACHEL, thought I was Kathleen.

Marcia had brought me every soap opera magazine she could find in the supermarket, and I was amazed at how little I knew about Kathleen Rafferty. I didn't know where these magazines got their information, but it wasn't from me; and I certainly wasn't having a relationship with WOODIE. And I swear I had never met Matt Dillon, even though our photos had been spliced together. That was entirely ficticious.

I hadn't realized how serious the serials were to people, who in a fever of addiction wouldn't dream of missing a single segment and clamored for any tidbit about the performers themselves. Actors, like Elisa Fairbairn who played DANIELLE, were as much shimmering, glimmering stars in the entertainment firmament as Lina Lamont had been in *Singing in the Rain*. Banana oil. It wasn't for me. But there I was being interviewed and coveted as though I were a really big deal.

"I understand you have a close personal relationship with Peter Searle who plays RACHEL's boyfriend, WOODIE, on the show. How do you manage to work, finish school and still maintain a relationship?"

I sighed.

"You're almost late, Kate," Ellin told me as I threw my coat on the counter of our dressing room.

"I know." I opened my pancake make-up and began to dab it on with a sponge. I'd been doing my own make-up for several weeks because I didn't trust Rhoda to make me look alive instead of like something that had just washed up on the shore.

"How'd it go?"

"Stupid. She had all these preconceived notions about

some fictional character named Kathleen Rafferty, and whenever I said something that didn't jibe, she'd ignore it. I could have stayed here for all the good it did to talk to her."

"I guess that's how it goes."

I looked at myself in the mirror. Damn simpering RACHEL. Today she was going to start changing. Usually all anyone used was gray eyeshadow and liner. I took my own umber pencil and made a smudgy line under my lower lashes. With the gray and the lights, my own coloring was being dissipated. I was going out there today looking like me.

"What are you doing?" Ellin asked as she wound her hair into a topknot.

"RACHEL's a drip. I'm fixing that."

"You know what that's going to look like on camera?"

"Me." I ran a darker gloss than usual over my lips. "Every day I'm powdered and faded out by those lights until I look as though I just had a life-and-death bout with consumption. I'm healthy, and from now on Rachel's going to be healthy, too. And she's not wearing any more of these dumb outfits!" I tossed the beige blouse across the room. "Little round pixie collars, I hate them. Puffy sleeves and cute bows. Yuck! I hate them!"

"Oh Kate . . ." Ellin moaned. "Lavinia's going to have a fit. Remember when Miriam wore her brown shoes. The screams echoed through the whole building. *Beige! Beige! Beige!*" Ellin mimicked Lavinia. "What's Gene going to say?"

" 'You're fired?' I can always hope." I stood and swirled the skirt to my dress in a wide circle.

We went to the set. With my boots on, I was a good six inches taller than Ellin and would tower above all the women. And I didn't care. For two months, I had been shot sitting or schlepping around in flat shoes. Enough was enough. My mother had always told me how wonderful it was to be tall and that I should carry myself proudly; but in the studio, the camera operators found I didn't fit into the frame alongside anyone else. RACHEL's stepmother, JANICE, was exactly five feet tall and teetered around the set on the highest heels available.

I felt the eyes of the cast and crew on me as I went to take my position in the hospital cafeteria where RACHEL was now working part-time after school. WOODIE was scheduled to meet her there, in one of the most popular gathering places in Riverford. There was the hospital cafeteria, the luncheonette, The Water's Edge Inn, The Ship's Rail and the HEGARTY kitchen. Big. Very big. If you sat in any one of those places, the whole world would eventually stroll past. Something like an American version of the Champs-Élysées.

For a moment, there was such total silence that my footsteps sounded like the sharp crack of rifle fire on an autumn day. Then I could hear Jack muttering to the stage manager.

"RACHEL!" Lavinia boomed over the intercom. "Why aren't you in costume?"

"This is RACHEL's costume," I replied looking squarely into number 2 camera, which was line on all the monitors.

"RACHEL doesn't wear clothes like that," Lavinia continued. "It's not in character."

"It is now," I said standing firm. Even I wasn't sure where I was finding the chutzpah to challenge the director, the very captain of our ship of soap.

"Oh let her wear it. It looks good," a voice came from the set next to the cafeteria.

"We're running late, Lavinia," Jack called.

"Wear it, but I want to see you after dress, RACHEL."

I smiled. Thank you, Fitch. If he hadn't spoken up, I wasn't certain Lavinia would have let it drop so quickly.

The dress rehearsal went smoothly, and we had a half

hour break before taping. On my way out of the studio, Lavinia pulled me aside into the sound control room.

"I know you're new to this, but we can't have someone deciding what their character will wear. RACHEL doesn't wear clothes like this." She flicked her hand across my sleeve.

The offhand gesture made me irritated and impatient. It was a beautiful dress, nothing outlandish, and RACHEL should have been proud to wear it. "Why don't you give RACHEL a chance to grow up a little."

"I'm the director. It's not the actor's job to tell the director how things will be."

"I'm not trying to tell you anything; I just think it's about time RACHEL began mainstreaming into Riverford life. She dresses like a character straight out of *Ma and Pa Kettle.*"

"That's an exaggeration. RACHEL's a very timid girl, and this dress would draw too much attention to her. It makes her look too exotic."

"If you wanted someone drab and colorless, why did you hire me? The last thing I am is plain."

"I didn't hire you," Lavinia replied coldly.

The implication of the remark hit me instantly. She didn't hire me and obviously hadn't approved of Gene's choice. Perhaps Gene and Roxanne hadn't even consulted her. A quick way to make an enemy.

"So take that dress off before taping," Lavinia continued.

I shrugged and walked out of the room. Fitch smiled encouragement as I turned the corner and headed for the stairs. Going up two flights, I went straight to Roxanne's office.

She looked up from her desk as I tapped on the doorjamb. "Hi, Kate. Come on in. What can I do for you?"

I stood in front of her for a moment. "What do you think of this dress?"

"It's beautiful."

"Lavinia doesn't want me to wear it for taping today."

Roxanne stopped smiling. "Let me get this straight. Is this your dress?"

"Yes."

"Uh-huh. Well . . ."

"Lavinia says RACHEL is too nondescript to wear something like this."

Roxanne was plainly uncomfortable at finding herself in the middle of a fight between Lavinia and me. "RACHEL is a shy person, getting over the sudden death of her mother, living in a new town, maybe she'd want to keep a low profile."

"Then why aim her at CAREY CROSS? She's going to want to be attractive for him, and ALISON certainly gets to dress decently. Shouldn't RACHEL try to keep up with her competition, I mean, assuming she is interested in CAREY, which she seems to be."

"I think her interest in CAREY is on the spiritual level."

"Of course she's not running in the same lane with CAREY and ALISON, she's just a naive little dope; but she thinks he could be interested in her. She hopes that he likes her. Besides, MILES is very wealthy and wouldn't let her out of the house in some of the rags she wears. Why doesn't JANICE take her out for a new wardrobe, and they can burn the junk she wore from Montana?"

"Okay, Kate, you've got me convinced. I'll explain it to Lavinia, and speak to Dave Dietz, too. He'll want to work some of these suggestions into the script."

"Thank you." I walked out of her office and felt terrific.

Eleven

Dear Rachel:

 After Friday's show, I think you should know what's been happening behind your back. CAREY CROSS has been giving ALISON uppers to help her study for her final exams. At night she has to take pills to sleep. He sells pills to all the kids at college because of the huge gambling debts he has run up, and is now talking to STAN, his supplier, about selling pills to the kids in high school. You may think CAREY is the nice guy he appears to be on the surface, but you are sadly mistaken. CAREY CROSS has no conscience, no ethics. All he wants is revenge. That's right, revenge. He's never forgiven his grandfather for throwing his mother out for marrying his father, and the CROSSES have no share of the REYDEL fortune. Just stick with WOODIE, and everything will be all right. WOODIE's in love with you. CAREY just wants to get you away from WOODIE for his own evil purposes, and if you have anything to do with him, I'm sure something terrible will happen. You're sure a nice person, but not too experienced, so you don't know how mean some people can be. Please take my warning seriously.

Your friend,
Betty.

Well, thank you, Betty. I folded the letter and placed it back in its distinctive pink envelope. The letters from Betty were the only ones I wanted to see, and Marcia sifted through all the mail to find them for me. Her one letter a week was all I had time for, and it was always worth a laugh or two.

My father entered the sun porch and stood for a moment looking out across the backyard. The sky was gray, but it wasn't snowing. He was still wandering aimlessly around the house as if he was searching for something to do, but he showed no enthusiasm or interest in anything. Being out of work was the worst thing that could have happened to him. I had never realized before how important acting was to him; it wasn't just a job, it was the wind that fanned his spark.

For me, it was just a job, and there was no spark to fan. The only good scenes were those with Fitch. I went through all the others without feeling, without being touched, running the gamut of emotions from A to B. For an actor, there is no showcase quite as wide as a serial; within a few months one actor can have amnesia, hysteria and become a religious zealot. I went through it all like a zombie.

Maybe it was a form of therapy. Instead of paying a psychiatrist, my father had always been able to get all his negative feelings out in front of a camera. Now he was lost, his only audience my mother, who was very tolerant but had her own things to do. Besides, she knew his routines too well and it wasn't so much fun for him to be on for her. They were too close; being on always required some distance from the audience to work well.

"Dad, did you ever have one fan who kept writing to you?"

He turned and it was almost as if he had to drag himself from his own thoughts to consider my question. "Years ago, when I had a run of about two years on a show called A TIME FOR US, I had a motherly sort of fan who wrote all the time." He sat in the rattan lounge chair. "Sometimes we think there's us, professionals in the business, and then there's them, the fans, and there's a world of difference between us. Once in a while you realize there's no difference, you're just doing something else for a living. I suppose there's something very intriguing about actors, and consequently they're sometimes elevated to a position higher than common folk. That's very dangerous because when you act you tell people stories about themselves, and if you can't see them, you can't be honest."

"It's not just a job, though."

"Um. I said for a living. I need to act, I've never known why. It came easily, comfortably, for me. When I act, I don't have to think about it. It's as if I suspend my disbelief in life. Everything else gets behind me—the bills, the disagreements, a cold, the weather, the world situation—everything fades. I need to get away. Maybe I'm not a strong person who can face everything unflinchingly."

He was being dramatic. I went over to sit on the edge of his chair.

"Everyone needs to forget for a little while. They need a way to escape. Some fans need to escape, too. We escape together."

I took his hand in mine. It was strong, and I could feel the calluses on the palms that had developed in the three months he had been doing the yard work.

"I think you're a stronger person than I am, Kate, and you'll go farther in this business than I will. You'll be the star of the Rafferty family because it's not so important to you."

"I don't want to be a star. I'd gladly give it all to you."

He smiled sadly. "It doesn't work that way. I don't care so much for being a matinee idol; I'd just like to keep working."

"I want to quit when my contract runs out."

"Because you don't want to hurt my feelings? We can't all be stars. There are a lot of talented people working in the business who aren't considered stars but are often better than those at the top. Grace Ransom for one."

"But what's going to happen to me!" I stood up and walked over to the rattan étagère filled with plants. "All these things keep happening to me that I don't deserve, that I haven't earned. I haven't paid my dues! Where's the struggle?"

"What do you mean you don't deserve this fine job and all the publicity?"

"Dad. Be honest. I can't act."

"Sure you can."

"Not like you. Not like Fitch. I say the lines but . . ."

"You're better than you know, and getting better all the time. I've been watching."

"It's a lie."

He paused for a moment, running his fingers down the leaves of the areca palm. "I had a short run on a show called OUR FIVE DAUGHTERS. This was a long time ago. It starred Esther Ralston. Have you ever heard of her?"

"No."

"She's one of these very grand women, stately, with a presence of royalty. She can carry herself so beautifully that it's awesome. Esther was a star of silent films in the twenties and that was a marvelous training ground. Today the silents can seem pretty funny and outdated; if the films are run at the wrong speed, they appear jerky and choppy. But if you see a good tinted print of something like *Street Angel,* it's incredible. Nothing we do today can compare with the subtlety. So there we all were, babies in the business compared with Esther, and we'd sit there, watching her hold the set for her own. I learned so much from watching her. And one day Esther's daughter, Judy, joined the cast. I came home and knew that someday I'd like to have a daughter to work with. I never wanted a son. I wanted a daughter."

"Dad . . ."

"Working with someone you love is . . . well, it was just a crazy idea. Just because you hope for something, doesn't mean it's going to happen. It's just something you think about fondly at times."

I didn't know what I could do about any of it.

He smiled. "So what do you want to do for Christmas? Anything special?"

"Would you mind if Fitch came up for the day?"

There was a questioning expression on his face.

"His family's in California, and we have to go back to work the next day. I just figured it would give him something to do."

"Is that all?"

"Why?"

"Just wondering. You know it's easy to get taken up by the atmosphere on the set."

"Yes?"

"I've seen you two together on the tube. There's something there, something going on."

"I don't know what it can be because all we are is friends."

He helped me finish the sentence and laughed. "That's the oldest line in the business. Well, the second oldest. The first is 'Don't call us, we'll call you.' "

"It's true."

"I'm not saying it has to be a romantic thing, but sometimes something clicks between two people and they really begin to transcend the material. Maybe that's what's going on."

Maybe it was inevitable that CAREY CROSS and RACHEL FERGUSON became enmeshed and embroiled, but it wasn't something I was looking forward to. When I thought about working with Fitch, it was more in terms of watching, not being out there with him. I couldn't keep up; I felt wooden and clumsy and still forgot my lines.

"Give him a call and invite him. I'd like to meet Fitch, one bad boy to another," he told me, standing. "I guess I'll go find your mother and see what we're having for dinner."

More wandering around the house, reduced to wondering what the next meal would offer.

I opened the drawer of the table beside the divan, pushed aside the phone book and took out the cast list, which contained everyone's phone number. I dialed and when the phone rang, I almost hung up, thinking I was making a mistake.

"Hello?"

"Fitch? This is Kate."

"Hi Kate. What's up?"

"I don't know what you're doing for Christmas Day, but if it's nothing, then you could come up here and have dinner with us. If you're doing something else, it's all right; I know you've probably made other plans already so don't feel badly when you say no."

"Kate . . ."

"Sure, well, that's okay. Maybe some other time. I just figured you might be alone. I don't know what made me think that."

"Kate. May I get a word in edgewise?"

"Sure. I'm sorry, it's just that I figured . . ."

"Enough already. I accept."

"What?"

"I'll come, and thank you for thinking of me."

We made the arrangements, and after I hung up, I sat there watching the sky grow darker until evening enveloped the room.

I still didn't know why I had invited him up for Christmas.

Twelve

My mother and I awoke early Christmas Day so we'd be able to put the turkey in the oven, make the pumpkin and apple pies, and do all the things we usually did before noon. Fitch was supposed to drive up around eleven, and I wondered if he'd make it each time I went past a window. The weather forecast was for snow, and I could practically see the snow hanging just over our heads in the sky waiting for the right moment to let go and inundate us.

I had made him a suede vest from some leather we had left over from a skirt my mother had once made. I wanted to give him something so that when we got things, he wouldn't feel left out. Even so, I was certain I had made a mistake in having him up for Christmas. New Year's Day would have been a better choice, more impersonal. Christmas was such a close, family-type holiday; he was bound to feel uncomfortable, no matter how nice we were. At least that's how I would have felt if I had been in his position. The only good thing about the day was that later we were going to have people in, after dinner, and if I ran out of things to talk about, these people could keep him busy for a few hours until it was time for him to head back to the city.

"Kate," my mother started as she opened the oven door to baste the turkey.

"Yes, Mom?" I finished washing the cooking utensils we had used for the pies.

"I'm just curious about this Fitch."

This Fitch. Okay. "Why?"

"I've seen him at the studio and on the show, but I don't know much about him."

"You know he's been in the business his whole life."

"Yes, but that's not exactly what I mean."

She was keeping carefully busy so she wouldn't have to face me as she tried to find out what was between us.

"He seems a little old for you."

"He reads older. He's just twenty-one."

"You're just a baby."

"I'm almost eighteen."

"So young."

So close to the age when Diana met Kerwin. "Mom, we're just friends."

"Well, Peter's your age, in high school, too. Fitch has finished college and is from Los Angeles. You've led a very sheltered life."

"No one but RACHEL FERGUSON has led a sheltered life. There is no such thing any more."

"I'm just wondering how serious you've become."

"Just because he's coming up for Christmas?"

"No. Because one day I sat down with your father and watched the show when you two were playing a scene."

"Mom, I can't believe you're saying this to me. You've been in the business. Did you get jealous every time Dad had to kiss some actress?"

"No, of course not."

"This is all acting. Fiction, remember? Make-believe."

"That just goes to show how much you know about it, Kate."

"What's that mean?"

"You can't act in a vacuum, with a blank slate. You get impetus from someplace."

"Fitch is a terrific actor."

"And you?" She asked as she briskly folded a kitchen towel then slipped it onto a wooden holder.

"I have a good imagination?"

"Lame excuse."

"Come on, Mom. This is craziness. If you didn't want me to get to know people like Fitch, you never should have sent me out to work."

"You just be careful."

"Who are you warning, me or RACHEL? Who's out to get me in his clutches? CAREY or Fitch?" I asked, then caught sight of a blue car pulling into the driveway. "Too late. He's here."

"We'll talk about this later."

"Sure we will," I replied as I ran up the back stairs to brush my hair and change.

Was I the only person who knew there was a difference between RACHEL and Kate? Everyone was starting to call me RACHEL, think of me as RACHEL, but I didn't live in Riverford. If an actor had to draw on personal experience to create a character, then RACHEL had to be some small part of me. Was I the simpering fool she was? I looked at myself in the bathroom mirror. For a moment, I couldn't tell who was looking back at me, because I saw the blank expression of RACHEL, who was forever being confounded by the big bad ways of the wicked world. When I stuck my tongue out at my reflection, I recognized Kate and breathed a sigh of relief. It was still me.

Maybe if I took Fitch's advice and brought more of myself to the part, I wouldn't feel as though I were living with a stranger. Maybe RACHEL would become a friend; I was just afraid she was my alter ego. What if I really was that naive, that simple, that vulnerable, and Kate was just a facade.

"Kate!" my father called up the stairs. "Fitch's here."

My stomach was strafed by a flurry of butterflies. "Okay. I'll be right there." Picking up the blouse I had decided to wear, I let it drop back on my bed. It wasn't right. In the past few months, I had acquired some nice things, but nothing seemed different. Then I found it way in the back, an eyelet cotton Victorian blouse I had made for a party last spring; I had spent hours inlaying strips of lace into it, so it was just like the ones the Gibson girls had worn at the turn of the century. I slipped it on and as I looked into the mirror, I saw Kate and felt much better. Everything had been going too fast, and I hadn't had enough time for me. Maybe RACHEL would rob a bank and get sent to a reformatory, and after June my life would return to normal.

Yet, if I didn't work on the show, I wouldn't see Fitch, unless I watched the show. And then he'd be CAREY CROSS, and Fitch wouldn't exist to me any more than Kate Rafferty existed to the viewers of LIFE TO ITS FULLEST. I could always write him fan letters. "Dear CAREY: I think you are very evil but very compelling. Why don't you give up pushing dope and settle down to the good life of being a nightwatchman and planting a vegetable garden by day? I once knew a girl from White Sulphur Springs; she was very boring . . ."

I went down the stairs and could hear my father and Fitch talking in the living room. Then I heard my father drop a log into the fire. By his voice, he sounded more cheerful than he'd been in a while, and I hoped seeing all his working friends who would commiserate with him wouldn't be too depressing.

As I came into the room, Fitch stood. I guess that was such an old-fashioned thing to do, I was caught off guard. That, and the fact that he was dressed impeccably in a tweed suit and sweater, made me just stop at the first step and look at him the way I did the first time I saw him on the set. I wondered at that moment if I would ever get used to him so that there wasn't the surprise, the sense of wonderment. It was the kind of surprise I had felt as a child when I still

82

believed in magic, in Santa Claus, flying reindeer. Fitch was actually in my living room.

"Hi."

"Hi, Kate."

I managed to walk over to the sofa without bumping into the coffee table for once and sat down.

Neither of us said anything for a moment, so my father asked if he could get us anything to drink. Fitch asked for a ginger ale. Then we were alone in the living room, the fire crackling and the snow beginning to dust the curled leaves of the rhododendrons outside.

"You look beautiful."

I blushed.

"That can't be the first time you've been told that."

"It doesn't count when it comes from your father."

In some ways you're very like RACHEL."

"Oh please," I groaned.

The snow had changed to ice crystals, and I could hear them striking the leaves.

"That might not be a bad thing."

My father came in and handed him the glass of soda. "So, Fitch, how do you like working for Gene?"

"I was meaning to talk to you about that."

My father raised his eyebrows with an actor's eloquence. "Maybe you have to go help your mother, Kate."

I looked back in surprise. "In other words, get lost?"

"For a few minutes before dinner. You don't want to hear about business, do you?"

"Do you?" I replied as I left. "Mom, Dad sent me here to help," I said as I entered the kitchen.

"You could put the relish tray in order."

I went to the refrigerator and began getting out jars of pickles, corn relish, a can of olives and some carrot sticks I had cut up earlier.

83

"He's very good looking."

"Fitch?" I asked.

"Of course, who else." My mother paused. "I suppose I can see how it would be natural for you to be . . . attracted to him. I just wish he had come later in your life. I think he's way beyond you."

"Don't get me confused with RACHEL."

"Something of you is RACHEL, and something of Fitch is CAREY."

The thought had crossed my mind more than once.

"Kate, there was something of your father in every character he played. Don't make the mistake of thinking that's not so."

I finished helping her in the kitchen, then began bringing food to the table, which was decorated with holly boughs we had cut from the trees out by the woods and pine cones we had gathered in the fall. As she lit the candles, I was reminded of the Christmas scene I had played two weeks ago in the FERGUSON dining room. The serials try to make the holidays very pretty with special decorations, poinsettias, and baubles of all sorts, but it hadn't compared with the Rafferty set.

My mother brought the turkey out and placed it in front of my father's seat; it was browned beautifully and glistened with a basting of butter. There were sprigs of parsley surrounding it on the platter and little spiced crabapples. The house was so silent, with only the clink of wine glasses being placed on the table and my mother in the kitchen, I felt almost as if time itself had paused. I knew at that moment, this Christmas was one I would remember for the rest of my life as the most special holiday we had ever spent together. If I lived to be eighty-eight and was confined to bed and all I could do was lie there and remember my past, this was the Christmas I would call to mind to comfort me. In other years maybe there would be very nice Christmases, with my own family, my own children, and I'd think back to the Christmas Day it snowed and my parents were with me. And Fitch.

Maybe by the time I was eighty-eight I wouldn't remember his name; all I'd remember was that he had had hair the color of the uppermost part of the candle's flame.

As I sat down across from my mother, I had to blink back the tears. I wanted nothing to change, and yet I knew that even within the hour it would all change and be gone forever. Fitch sat next to me, and I could smell the warm gingerbread smell of him. Every time I would smell that spicy sweet scent, I would remember just that instant when my father began to cut into the turkey. It was so vivid that a photograph could not have given me a more clear picture of the scene.

Everyone made small talk about this and that and the next thing, while I just sat there, pretending to eat when all I was doing was drinking in every detail, storing it for the future, for a time when I would need a sad, sweet moment like this. Then we finished the main course, had coffee and pie and went into the living room again. The snow was coating the rhododendron with a thick layer of white.

My mother handed everyone their presents, modest ones, and the box for Fitch. He seemed surprised but not uncomfortable; but then he was a good enough actor to hide anything. I opened my packages, and I suppose I showed appropriate delight, but I was far more interested in watching everyone else.

My father seemed content. Maybe he wasn't totally happy, but I hope he wasn't pretending to be enjoying himself. My mother was gracious and charming and adored the little china coalport cottage my father had given her.

Fitch opened his present and lifted out the vest with almost as much care as if it had been made of cobwebs.

"Kate made that," my father said proudly.

"I hope it fits," my mother added. "If it's too big, we can take it in. If it's too small . . ."

"Go on a diet." My father laughed.

"Thank you, Kate," Fitch said to me.

I nodded. It was all I could do.

"You know, as an Angelino, I don't have much experience with snow. How about taking me for a walk?"

"Sure, that's a good idea," my mother prompted.

I went to the front hall closet to get my sheepskin coat, and as I pulled on my boots, my father handed Fitch a pair of his rubberized hunting boots and his red mackinaw.

We stepped off the porch into almost four inches deep and began walking toward the road.

"Show me where you go to think," he told me.

"How do you know there is such a place?"

"Isn't there?"

"Yes."

We crossed a stone wall and began tramping through the field next to our house, walking and climbing up the hill until we got to the very top. On the large rock in the stone wall there, I could sit and let the wind blow my head clear. Today the snow wet my face and caught on my eyelashes. The surrounding hills were gray with thick clouds and snow heavy in the air.

"Do you remember the first time we talked?"

"Yes."

"You said you were Just Kate, not Kathleen."

"That's right."

"Well, Just Kate, I have a present for you. I saw it and was reminded of you." Reaching in his pocket, he removed a small square brown leather box and handed it to me.

I looked at him.

"Open it."

By its shape, I knew what was inside. I pressed a small button and the top flipped back revealing the most beautiful ring I had ever seen. It was round, surrounded by little tiny diamonds and a red stone in the very center.

"It's white gold; the stone is a spinel."

"Fitch . . ."

"Try it on, maybe it won't fit. It's quite old. This is the original box. The man said the ring was in pristine condition. Can you imagine it's over sixty years old and never been worn? You have to wonder why."

I slipped it onto the fourth finger of my right hand, and it fit perfectly.

"I guess you could call it a friendship ring."

At that moment, he was so dear to me that I knew I had been swept away and a part of me had been stolen.

"Hey, Just Kate, why are you crying?" he asked and held me close.

"I don't know. Maybe I'm afraid." Afraid that this moment would end and knowing there could never be another quite like it in the rest of my life. And afraid that my mother was right, and he was way beyond me.

He held me tight, and the snow began to cover us just as if we were part of the hill.

Thirteen

AFTER CHRISTMAS the atmosphere on the set changed. To me the smiles seemed strained, the conversations forced and the tension crackling like lightning in an August thunderstorm. Rumors spread like wildfire, changed daily like the headlines of a newspaper. We were going to be cancelled, shortened, fired, lengthened, moved to another time slot, expanded, cut back; and the older family members threatened to quit because they had been pushed into the background by the newer cast members.

I didn't know what the truth was; I was only worried about the story line calling for WOODIE to become ever more ardent with RACHEL. Peter was all right, but I didn't want to get into any clinches with him. So far RACHEL was being shy with WOODIE and fairly flirtatious with CAREY, who could only be described as having a distant bemused tolerance for her.

Actually, that really wasn't my main worry. I was beginning to remember September 26 all over again. Everyone's contracts were coming up for renewal soon, at least the new members on their thirteen-week runs. If the show was in trouble, some people might be dropped. If CAREY CROSS was shot by some mob hit man because he didn't turn in his drug money or was going to turn state's evidence, then he'd be shot and come under the knife of MILES FERGUSON, surgeon supreme. But MILES was becoming an alcoholic as a result of his deteriorating marriage, and heaven only knew what he would do with a scalpel in his hand if he was loaded on the vodka neats (water) he drank continually. CAREY'd get shot, sent to Riverford Hospital and goodbye Fitch. With MILES as a surgeon, he wouldn't have a chance. Roxanne broke the news during the first week of January that five of us were to be featured in *Outlook*, a personality magazine that wanted to explore the cast members who were causing LTIF's ratings to soar. During Christmas, Roxanne explained, the ratings had exploded because the younger audience had been home, and with nothing else to watch had tuned in and had liked what they had seen. Mail was flooding in and even phone calls, which was unusual. The network was ready to commit itself to almost anything to continue the new trend.

The five to be featured were WOODIE, FONDA, CAREY, RACHEL and ALISON. We were all slightly mystified and felt varying degrees of elation over the situation. All of us that is but ALISON. Since ALISON had become involved with CAREY and had been taking pills to stay awake and be bright and vivacious, the absolute darling of Riverford had been getting progressively more difficult to deal with. I didn't care much how I was lit or from what side. I figured Lavinia and the technical crew knew what they were doing far better than I; but Deanna, being the ripe old age of twenty-three, knew better than everyone. She had a side. When you have to play a scene with someone who refuses to have the right side of her face toward the camera, it can become pretty aggravating. Then she'd change her lines. I'd get lost listening to one of her monologues; it was like playing a game of blindman's buff to find my cue. Fitch didn't care because he was able to twist the dialogue back to suit him before she knew what had happened to her.

When ALISON and CAREY kissed, ALISON had to have her face toward the camera, never CAREY. This went on to such a noticeable degree, my father mentioned it to me and told me it was inevitable. Men are second-class citizens in the world of the daytime serial. Women are strong, ambitious, motivated people. Women get all the best scenes to play. Men may be scoundrels or warm, loving fathers, but they are never very interesting and they never receive the publicity the actresses do. Even so, Deanna was having a hard time keeping Fitch in his get-thee-behind-me role. To hear her talk, the article was only about her. And having her placed right in the center of the photo for the magazine cover, flanked by the two brunettes, me and Ellin, did nothing to hinder her intention of playing the star to the hilt.

After the shoot, Fitch and I left the fancy photography studio to have dinner at a small rathskellar downtown, a dark restaurant, in a basement with almost undiscernible photos of famous patrons hung on the yellowed walls. My ring caught what little light there was and made sparkles on my hand. I was wearing it all the time, except as RACHEL, and I'd only take it off for the taping.

"I think I'm beginning to miss L.A." Fitch told me after the German-accented waiter took our order.

I couldn't have been more surprised if Greta Garbo sat down at the table next to us. My stomach betrayed me again, twisting as it had the first and last time I had ridden a roller coaster.

"I've never spent a winter in the snow."

The snow was filthy brown slush in the streets, three and four inches deep. When the snow was falling, New York could be incredibly beautiful. The next day, it was a mess.

"Are you trying to tell me something?"

"No."

I didn't say anything.

"You know that Lavinia and I haven't been getting along very well lately. Deanna's been complaining, too."

"Are you serious?"

He nodded.

"What's her problem? She got her face in the center position today. What next? The cover of *TV Guide?*"

"She thinks she's on her way up and I'm detracting from her."

"And . . ."

"So the story line is going to be changed."

"I don't believe it. Since when does a nobody like Deanna dictate to the producers and writers."

"Since she got hot to the media. Since the ratings went up. Since those producers and writers will do anything to save their necks."

"So what story line are you getting?"

"What difference does that make. I just think that the combination of all these things makes me rather an undesirable commodity. I don't think they're going to pick up my contract."

I didn't have to ask how he knew or if he was sure. My father could always smell it when the wind changed direction, too.

"Look on the bright side."

"There's a bright side?" I asked.

"We'll be playing a lot of scenes together. From now on RACHEL is to be the proud recipient of all CAREY CROSS's attentions."

I moaned. Even with the ring, my Edwardian friendship ring, whatever friendship meant, I still didn't know what was going on between Fitch and me. I felt there was a bond of some kind, but I had no way of knowing if he felt it or if it was only in my imagination.

When my mother said I was just a baby, I really was. It wouldn't take much for me to get caught up in something I really didn't understand, thereby making a fool of myself and making a couple of people pretty miserable in the bargain. Knowing CAREY CROSS, RACHEL was in for a hot time in the old town tonight, sweetheart. I wasn't so sure that under those circumstances I could keep a line drawn between what was happening to RACHEL and what was happening to Kate.

"You've only been here a couple of months," I said.

"Yeah, I know. Time flies when you're working for scale." Fitch smiled.

"Not funny."

"It's not so bad."

First my father, now Fitch. I hated this business. I wanted out. Why couldn't RACHEL be run over by JANICE as she drives the car leaving MILES? I didn't want to be on the cover of any personality magazine. I didn't want a photo of me spliced with one of Pete in a fan magazine saying that our engagement was imminent and was planned to coincide with the engagement of RACHEL and WOODIE. (All lies.) I didn't want Fitch to lose his job and get all depressed like my father.

Only for the superstars was anything different. The majority of actors were just itinerant performers with a traveling troupe. Jobs were transient. People lived out of suitcases, ready to hop a bus or a train or a plane to someplace else like in the old days of vaudeville.

Of course, since he was pulling in a salary something like mine, Fitch could have bought six or seven first class tickets back to L.A. and not have felt it in the bank account at all. Not to mention Buddy Whosit Boy Space Cadet's residuals, which poured in like clockwork. Fitch wouldn't be sticking his thumb out alongside Route 80 waiting to be picked up by a semi traveling to the coast for lettuce.

The waiter brought our food, but I had completely lost my appetite.

"It'll be all right."

I didn't see how that was possible. Everything was going faster and faster. Maybe I should just take it as part of the business, I told myself. As life in Riverford flowed with unexplicable turns of events, so then did real life. Tomorrow something else would happen. New characters would enter from stage left. Others would exit. That was how the play went. All I had to do was get used to that idea.

Fourteen

"ALL RIGHT, WOODIE AND RACHEL, we're going to come in from the front of the car and see you two sitting there. WOODIE you lean over. Say your line. Then kiss RACHEL." Lavinia was directing from her podium.

I got into the passenger seat of the car on the set. It didn't have a windshield because all that glass would reflect too much light and make burn spots in the cameras. I didn't want Pete touching me, but RACHEL was going to have to sit there and take it.

Pete got in and smiled at me.

"RACHEL, you pull back slightly. Then WOODIE, I want you to touch her face, trace down her cheek with one finger and then go to her top button."

I looked at Lavina in surprise. That wasn't in the script.

"I was just on the phone with Dave, and we're fixing this scene now. Then WOODIE, kiss her more intently, RACHEL you'll pull back and say your line. Got it?"

Got it? Are you kidding me? I was silently screaming in protest.

"Ready? Three two one. Hit it."

"RACHEL," WOODIE said as he turned the car engine off. Behind us were the faked twinkling lights of Riverford. "You really look beautiful tonight."

He kissed me, and I had to keep myself steeled so I wouldn't flinch. Then I pulled back slightly. "Do you really think so? I wanted to dress up for the party, knowing your whole family would be there. CAREY is a very good dancer, don't you think?"

"I don't want to talk about my cousin," WOODIE said as he brought his hand up to my face, then began trying to trace a line down my cheek. I say try because he was fumbling and touching me as if I had whatever slime the old man in *The Blob* had had all over him just after Steve McQueen and Aneta Corseut found him in the woods.

"WOODIE," Lavinia called. "You can do better than that. You are being overcome by your passions, remember?"

Ol' WOODIE tried it again and succeeded in giving me a good poke in the ear.

Fitch's unmistakable laughter rang out from the other end of the studio where he was watching on the monitor.

"Okay, WOODIE, now go to the blouse. You try to unbutton it."

"What?" I asked.

"Don't worry. We'll slash cut before anything can be seen."

Great. That's a big relief.

WOODIE began fumbling with my blouse.

"Come on, Romeo," Lavinia said impatiently. "Surely you've done this before."

WOODIE blushed.

I was practically paralysed. It was every bit as horrible and real as if I were actually on top of some Lover's Leap with a guy I didn't like and who was trying to put the make on me. I had to restrain myself from jumping out of the car and trying to walk home. It was that or smash this dim-o in the head with my pocketbook. Maybe in that respect RACHEL and I had something in common; neither of us had had this experience in our lives. And I suppose if we had had a choice, we would have opted for CAREY/Fitch instead of WOODIE/Pete.

95

Dear RACHEL:

You should know CAREY CROSS told his close friend, STAN, that he's going to get you away from his cousin. He made a joke out of being the teacher and you being his student . . .

Betty, why are you warning me about CAREY when it's WOODIE who's giving me such a hard time, I wondered as I winced when WOODIE's shirt button caught on the lace of my blouse.

"Okay, Romeo. Practice. LOUISE, are you ready?" Lavinia walked off.

Pete leaned in to practice, and I gave him a shove. "Not now, buster. I'm taking a break."

I walked into the lavatory and sat on the edge of the sink, twisting my ring around and around my finger. If I had to play that scene at all, I wanted to do it with Fitch. It didn't seem right having Pete hanging all over me.

Ellin walked in and looked at me.

"I think I must be hopelessly old-fashioned or something," I told her.

"Why?"

"How do I even explain it. Because I don't think I like the concept of kissing and everything with Pete."

"Oh, Kate."

"Oh Kate, what?"

"You're really getting fixated on him, aren't you?"

"No. Of course not."

Ellin tried not to smile but wasn't very successful.

"Maybe that's what it is. I'm fixated on him. I don't know what else it could be, but it's driving me crazy. I don't want to say or do anything to disturb the relationship we have."

"But you're not very happy with the way things are."

I paused. "I guess I'm not but what else could there be."

"That's tough. It happened to me once."

"And? And? Don't keep me in suspense."

"And nothing happened."

"That's what I figured."

"He's back in Somerset, Virginia, just where I left him. Not that I left him, I just left. There was New York and my career, and sometimes people just don't come together. Maybe the stars aren't right. If things are supposed to work out, they will. Sometimes I believe that. That's my advice, and I wouldn't count on his being around much longer, either."

"Why?"

"Well, dearie, you're preoccupied but talk has it that the powers that be may find it expeditious to abandon CAREY CROSS. Deanna isn't very happy with Fitch and neither is Lavinia. When you lose the support of your peers, you're in real trouble. He's just a little too confident, too secure. People don't trust him. CAREY CROSS was originally nothing like the person he is now; then he was struggling to be accepted. He was little more than a walk-on until Fitch began very competently to manipulate Dave Dietz and Lavinia until the character changed. He was right on target because the audience adores CAREY at the same time they're hating him. Some people would think that kind of input was great, and good for the show. Lavinia finds it very naughty of Fitch."

"I guess that all went right by me. Suppose I'll ever wake up?"

Ellin hugged me. "If I'd received that ring from a guy like Fitch, I wouldn't ever want to wake up."

We started back to the studio, but I stopped at the telephone. "I'll be there in a minute. I have to make a call." I almost ran back to my dressing room, grabbed my change purse, then ran back to the pay phone. I slipped a dime in and dialed.

It rang a few times and the operator came on. "That will

be one dollar and seventy cents for the first three minutes."

It wiped out almost all my change and then the phone rang at the other end.

"Hello?"

"Dad."

"Kate? Where are you? What's wrong?"

How did he know something was wrong? "I'm at the studio. Dad, I hate this business."

"So do I."

"What are you talking about? You love this business."

"I love acting. I hate the business." He paused. "Maybe it wasn't such a good idea for us to push you into it when it wasn't something you really wanted. I'm sorry."

"If I'm here and unhappy, it's my fault. I don't want you to be sorry."

"Are you unhappy?"

"I'm too crazed to know if I'm not happy. They change the script three times before we shoot, and now they're dumping me into romantic scenes with drippy WOODIE."

"What does Fitch think about it?"

I didn't know because he didn't say anything about it, and why should it matter to him. I was just a passing acquaintance, a little actress who lived in Connecticut where it snowed. He'd remember me that way when he was back in California. If he remembered me at all.

"Seventy-five cents, please." The operator interrupted my silence.

"I don't have any more change, Dad. I'll see you later. Probably tomorrow, if we ever get through taping."

"Take care, Kate."

"Bye."

I started back toward the studio. RACHEL was in love with CAREY. At least she thought she was; being the naive little drip she was, she couldn't see straight. The minute the dashing CAREY CROSS paid the slightest amount of attention to her, she fell apart, melted all over the Riverford Hospital Cafeteria.

With RACHEL, it was the temptation of exact opposites, the forbidden candy, the lure of danger. CAREY was the high wire RACHEL was afraid to walk, yet she was mesmerized by the thrill it offered. She was so dumb she thought someone like CAREY CROSS could actually be interested in her.

The studio door closed softly behind me, and the set was very still. When a scene was being done, it was almost impossible to hear the words, because we only spoke loud enough for the mikes to pick up our voices. The rest was swallowed in the cavern.

By reflex I glanced up at the monitor. CAREY CROSS was kissing ALISON.

I thought we were ending that story line! And Marcia had showed me the new *Daystars* Magazine with a little blurb in the general news/gossip column. "Lovely Deanna Davison, ALISON REYDEL of LTIF, has found a new beau in castmate Fitch Cooper, CAREY CROSS, the resident bad boy of Riverford. Will we be hearing wedding bells soon?"

It made me furious. So furious I didn't take my eyes off the monitor, tripped over a camera cable about the size of a boa constrictor and fell into Bill the stage manager.

"SSSSSHHHHHH!" The A.D. hissed at me.

In November when the copy had been written for *Daystars,* Fitch and Deanna were practically strangers. It was a fabrication. I knew he thought she was unprofessional and untalented, but my gut reaction was a strong desire to tear her hair out, every bleached strand. That was the real Kate. Straightforward. Impulsive. Foolish.

Some people can take scraps and make them into a banquet. I was being handed the dream of hundreds, maybe thousands of girls across the country. I was becoming a star.

I led a fascinating, romantic life. Reporters wanted to know what I thought. I was being surrounded by handsome and glamourous people. My manager was looking for movie properties for me.

But I was Just Kate, who had the talent for taking a banquet and turning it into scraps.

Fifteen

RACHEL's FAVORITE PLACE TO SIT and think was on a dock overlooking the river. For a few days CAREY watched her behavior patterns and knew exactly where she'd be at any given time, planning how he would begin to make a serious move on her.

The dock was a raised platform in the studio with a backdrop showing water and sailboats in the distance. A few small trees were nailed to holders to make it all seem more realistic. And as RACHEL became progressively more confused, she'd bundle up against the winds that blew off the water and stand on this dock, tears being fairly whipped into her eyes.

"Three two one. Hit it."

RACHEL stood there, totally disconsolate. MILES had forbidden her to have anything to do with CAREY because they had been seen together in the hospital cafeteria the previous day. On top of that, she had heard via the Riverford grapevine (a mini-UPI) that CAREY was dealing in substances that were highly illegal. She didn't believe that. Not CAREY. But then again, ALISON had acted rather bizarre at the party and had had to be brought upstairs to her bedroom. After all, CAREY didn't have a job, and everyone in town knew they were practically destitute, those CROSSES; yet he did have money and wonderful clothes and a fancy sportscar. It was clear even to RACHEL that he was getting money from someplace.

"RACHEL?"

RACHEL whirled around to find CAREY behind her.

"Hi, darlin'. What are you doing out here? You'll freeze."
CAREY put his arms around RACHEL.

The set was painted mostly in shades of gray, and his eyes took on the color of winter water.

"I'm up," I said.

There was an audible sigh from behind the cameras, followed by, "How did you know I was here?"

"How did you know I was here?" RACHEL asked.

"I know all kinds of things," he replied.

"I've been hearing some stories about you."

"Well, darlin', you can't believe everything you hear."

RACHEL paused to give one of her tortured expressions. "Have you been giving ALISON . . . pills?"

CAREY was a cool customer and didn't even blink. "Who told you that?"

"I just heard it somewhere. It doesn't matter where."

"It matters to me. I come from a good family, and it hurts our reputation as outstanding citizens to have rumors like this flying around town. And besides, RACHEL, I wouldn't want you to think I was that kind of person, involved with that kind of thing."

"Then it's a lie."

"Of course it's a lie," CAREY lied.

"I didn't want to believe it but . . ."

"Rumors can appear to be more real than the truth itself. If you have a question about me, I want you to come straight to me, 'cause RACHEL, I'll always tell you the truth."

Then slowly, gently, CAREY put his hands on RACHEL's face and drew her closer to him. Lavinia had told us to milk it for all it was worth, really build up the tension. I saw the tally light on camera 2 fade so camera 3 could take a close-up of our faces for the big moment.

The butterfly brigade attacked again.

And he kissed me. The script didn't say brotherly this time, and it wasn't.

Then the cameras were rolling down to the next set for the next scene. Everyone walked away.

Fitch smiled. I tried to smile back.

RACHEL was so stupid.

Damn.

Two weeks later, I was sitting in a red chair, having my hair done, listening to Ozi tell Antonio how he had done Kate Hepburn's hair some time or other. Antonio had done Lauren Bacall. And they were trading Hollywood stories left and right. On the television, which was perpetually on, LTIF had just returned from a commercial break and I glanced in the mirror to see myself standing on the dock, with a winter coat, scarf and hat, sweltering under the studio lights.

I heard the first few vague familiar notes of music, which I had heard elsewhere but couldn't quite place, sort of sad sounding, slow and rolling. It fit how I felt perfectly. As Ozi stepped away for a moment, I spun the chair around to watch the set.

It was me. It was RACHEL on the dock. Was that what I looked like? But it didn't seem like me. Then CAREY came into the scene, and the music faded as he began to speak.

Fitch came into the room. "Hi."

"Hi."

I watched us together on the set. It hadn't looked like that. Normal people live their lives without flashbacks. They never see again what they've done. There are no retakes in real life. But I was watching my disembodied self experience something that had happened two weeks before. Normal people don't have to deal with splitting themselves into pieces and being shown the disparate sections under the microscopic eye of the camera.

It seemed to me as if those silent moments between RACHEL and CAREY lasted almost indefinitely. The same music welled up again, building as Carey reached over to kiss RACHEL. The camera paused, caressed the people on the dock, then faded, leaving only a few notes of music as a remembrance.

There was a hoot from down the hall. STAN maybe.

"Phew!" Ozi said. "I'm going to be working on an X-rated soap, if you two keep up like this."

I just wanted to be alone.

"Looks like we've got us a theme song," Fitch said as he came in and sat down in the chair next to me.

"A theme song?"

"Sure. Everyone has music to match their character. VIOLET has something soft and slightly old-fashioned. MILES has something strong. RACHEL has something sweet and uncomplicated. But now we have something that's all ours. And it really blows me away."

"Why?"

"Have you ever heard that song before?"

"It sounds familiar."

"It was just released. It's called 'Set You Free'."

"That's right, I've been hearing it on the radio."

"Me, too. It's by Whelan Cooper."

"Sure. I've heard of him."

"He's my older brother, and I brag on him whenever I get the chance. We share a house when he's not on tour." Fitch smiled. "It sure is funny how his song was picked as our theme. Boy, if they knew Whelan was my brother . . . but you have to figure the television division knows nothing about what's going on in the record division. They just picked a song destined to be a hit."

Roxanne rushed into the room. "Did you see it?"

I nodded. "So?"

She rushed to the end of the room, then paced to the

door and retraced her steps back again. "The chemistry!"

"Hey, Roxanne," Ozi said. "You'd better watch it or you'll have the censors and their scissors after you," he teased.

"The switchboard is lighting up! We haven't gotten this many calls since DANIELLE was raped by DEREK. Of course, we all know how DEREK was. He . . ."

"I don't remember that," I said coldly. My father had never done that.

"It was five years ago, when he first came on the show," Roxanne explained.

Rape, incest, murder, violence, sorrow, disease, birth and death were all homogenized and boiled down to how many ratings points they were worth. We moved from one concept to another, chewing subjects over until they had given up all the Neilsens and ARBS they were worth, and then we shot to another topic. But we never got to the heart of the matter. Everything was shallow, distant, casual. Nothing was handled realistically. Or as in real life. Riverford had zip in common with real life. It was sterilized and fictionalized and dramatized until it bore no relation to truth.

Yet people believed it. I received letters every week from fans who poured out their hearts and minds to RACHEL FERGUSON as if she could help them. People believed that somewhere there was a Riverford. It wasn't their life, but it was someone's life.

And it was someone's life. It belonged to Dave Dietz and his crew sitting at their typewriters, furiously trying to keep their jobs by hooking the audience, addicting them to a fairy tale. Only by doing this could they work, could we all work. Our real life was to pretend we lived in this fantasyland where a myriad of bad things kept happening to us, but never really touched us to the core. We cried, those who could, those who couldn't got the bottle of glycerin tears for the length of a shot. After that, we went back to another script and maybe a cold dinner because taping ran late.

I was RACHEL. I was the character I played to many people. But in real life, I was just Kate. What no one seemed to understand, not the people who came up to me in Bloomingdale's or the Stop-and-Shop or those who wrote letters, those who warned me about CAREY (thank you, Betty), those who wanted to get into show biz, too, so they could be a glamourous star like me, was that there is no real life. There's just life. My real life was playing a part and being Kate Rafferty and trying to finish high school by correspondence and wondering where I was going. Just like a lot of people.

I had someone come up to me on Fifth Avenue who grabbed my hand and began pumping it wildly. "My friends are going to die with envy," she told me. "I actually met you in real life." When people watch television, they get the impression that the people they see there live something other than real lives.

Four or five times a week now I was being brought electronically into hundreds of thousands of homes. Maybe millions. I didn't pay attention to numbers. And somehow on that tiny screen, I was being magnified until I was larger than life, and the publicity mills made us all grist for their grindstones. Television was this ever-hungry behemoth that swallowed everyone up—actors, writers, producers, viewers— we all went to feed its appetite, to keep the system going. We needed the viewers, and they needed us. We needed a common fix, and I knew what it was. It was so simple and so obvious I wondered why it hadn't occurred to me before. Hype makes the world go round.

Who wants reality when you can have something better, something perfect and painless, something that doesn't require participation, just requires spectators. And to that end, the system will eat you up and spit you out when it's done with you. And after it rolls over you, you can sit there in the middle of the road while you watch the forty-foot-long tractor trailer disappear down Route 66, staring uncomprehendingly, wondering what to do next.

I had seen that look on my father's face, and it had practically broken my heart. I'd never let that happen to me. But I wasn't sure I could put the brakes on before it did.

And now the producers were talking about trashing Fitch, to leave him by the roadside, maybe wondering what he'd do next.

"Kate?" Roxanne asked.

I looked up. "What?"

"Where were you? Haven't you heard a word I said?"

No. And I didn't suppose I missed much.

"Gene's going to be very happy about how this is working out. He wanted a story line that would really stir up interest, and we've got a winner here," Roxanne said as she walked out the door.

I looked at Fitch. He didn't seem very elated by this all. Fact was, he was no happier than I, and I was downright gloomy.

He shrugged almost imperceptibly then stood. "My brother said something to me once. The door of opportunity swings both ways. Sometimes it can open. Other times it swings back and smacks you in the face. Unfortunately you can never tell which it's going to be. So he wrote a song that had a verse, 'I've got nothing to lose, so I'll go for it all. Later I'll know how much it cost.'" His smile was so thin you could have shone a light through it.

I watched him leave, and then I heard the clinking of change being fed into the phone, clanging like a one-armed bandit.

My father was waiting for me in the living room when I got home at ten. The fire was still going in the fireplace, and he motioned me over to sit next to him on the sofa, like a little girl again.

"What seems to be the problem, Kate?"

"On Christmas Day, Fitch and you had a private conversation. What did he want?"

"Well, he wanted some advice."

"How to deal with the tricky triumvirate?"

"Basically yes. He wonders if they'll be picking up his contract."

I pushed some hair behind my ear. "He told me that."

"Are you having any trouble with Lavinia or Gene?"

"No, everyone's pretty nice."

"I saw your scene with Fitch today."

I waited for him to continue, but he didn't. "I saw it too, and the switchboard lit up and Roxanne came down ranting and raving about ratings and success. I couldn't help but think that maybe they'll pick up his contract because he's so convincing and no one could replace him. You know, 'the part of CAREY CROSS will now be played by Milton Dumpkopf'. If it's such a good story line and all . . . well, he's carrying me. Playing a scene with WOODIE is like torture. But with Fitch, I'm bound to look good because he hands me everything tied up in a neat bundle. Anyone would look good with him."

"I think you're underestimating yourself, Kate. Maybe that was true in the beginning, but today I really began to notice a change."

"It's because of Fitch. You'll see, after he goes, I'll look like a schlunk again. Do you think Gene might change his mind?"

He sighed. "Knowing Gene as well as I do, I'd have to say no. To him, an actor is simply a piece of merchandise, replaceable, expendable. Women are slightly more valuable, but if they cause enough trouble, they go, too."

"So I guess I should just grow up and expect Fitch to be leaving soon," I said.

"Do you think you're in love with him?"

I don't know why I was so surprised at the question, but I was so shocked for a moment, I couldn't speak. "I don't know what I think. And whatever it is, it's in my imagination."

"How so?"

"Fitch has always been just a good friend. The ring is a friendship ring. We eat together, shop together, go to the park together, work together. We're spending about twelve hours a day together; and when he goes, I'm really going to miss him. But it's as if he's my big brother."

"I didn't realize that. I suppose I thought. . ."

"It was more than that?"

"Yes. But Kate, it's really rather curious. When I saw the scene today, and I'm talking objectively, as a professional watching two professionals, there was an added dimension there. I would have sworn to it. There's chemistry there."

"Roxanne said that. I don't know anything about this chemistry business. I know I feel a bond, but I don't know if it's there for him. I just know that when he goes, if he goes, there'll be unfinished business. Am I making any sense at all?"

"You're making excellent sense, and it makes me feel very old. I can see my little girl's growing up. I hope it works out for you. Just go with care. Sometimes it may be difficult to just do nothing, but if you feel the balance is precarious, maybe that's the best thing to do."

I nodded. RACHEL could blow it with CAREY, but I wasn't stupid.

"You'll work it all out. I have plenty of confidence in you."

I wished I had his confidence in my abilities, but maybe I was preoccupied. The door was starting to swing, and I was getting ready to be smacked in the face on its way back.

Sixteen

"YOU'VE BEEN GETTING a lot of requests to start a fan club."

I started to choke on the tea I was drinking. "Marcia. This has got to stop!"

She opened the manila envelope and dumped a bunch of letters on the kitchen table. "These people want to join your fan club."

"I don't want a fan club."

"Everybody has a fan club."

Marcia was beginning to know more about the business than I did. She was organized and kept track of everything for me, including clipping all references to me in the fan magazines. Without her, I would have been totally ignorant of what was going on around me. Without her, I would have thrown all the scripts away; but she saved them in marked boxes in the basement for future reference. She tried to reply to all the letters I received; with her, it was as if there were two Kates. She was my clone.

"My father never had a fan club, and he survived."

My mother walked into the kitchen. "He most certainly did, and he still has loyal fans."

"And," Marcia continued, "you've been invited to attend a soap opera convention in a shopping mall called Severance Center in Ohio."

"I don't want to attend any conventions. Isn't there some rule that says when all this stops being fun, I get to quit?" I asked.

"I never heard that rule before," my mother replied as

she stuck her finger in the spider plant pot, then gave it a glass of water.

But it hadn't really been fun. Acting with Fitch had made it worthwhile, but when he left, there'd be nothing.

"You're getting a lot of positive mail about this story line with CAREY. They want to see you two together."

"Good. They'll like it even better when they see what happens in two weeks."

Today, CAREY had followed WOODIE and RACHEL back to the REYDEL mansion and had watched through the window while WOODIE tried to make another of his unsuccessful moves on RACHEL. The next morning, CAREY caught up with RACHEL as she walked to school and really turned on the charm faucets. Of course, little RACHEL became flustered and uncomfortable, practically scuffing her toes in the dirt, then trotted off to school on cloud fifteen after he gave her a goodbye kiss.

I was beginning to hate the story line. I felt it was a cheap shot to get ratings by titillating the audience and using me to do it. When the mail response went up, Dave socked it in harder. If this much is good, more is even better. It might have been interesting to the audience, but for the past six weeks I'd been doing basically the same thing, juggling CAREY and WOODIE four times a week and getting nowhere.

Time on a soap bears no relation to real time. A child can grow up within a year. Or it may take a year to resolve something it normally would have taken three weeks. But because we had the audience hooked on this concept, we were going to stay with it, crawling. LIFE creeps at its petty pace, tomorrow and tomorrow and so forth.

I had no idea where it would all end. We were never told. I never gave up the hope that CAREY would become indispensable; but even our spy, Roxanne's secretary, Hilary, who was very willing to talk with Marcia, had no idea what the plans were for Fitch. Marcia was always very careful when she went fishing for information because we didn't want anyone to know we were interested.

"Here's your latest letter from Betty," Marcia said handing it to me.

"It's Betty time, Mom."

"Okay, okay," my mother replied and sat at the table with a cup of tea in her hand. "Read it out loud. We're ready."

Dear RACHEL:

I still haven't figured out why you want to get involved with CAREY CROSS. He's into the mob and if you keep going the way you are, you'll become the kind of low-life he is. Why don't you get smart and stick with WOODIE, a nice boy. Go to college, get engaged to WOODIE and marry him. You'll live in the REYDEL mansion and have a good life. Why throw it all away for a nogoodnik like CAREY? I can understand there's some kind of physical attraction or something, but just ignore it. If you don't see him, you'll get over it soon. Can't I say anything to convince you of this terrible mistake you're making? Could I come to Riverford and try to talk you out of it? Or maybe you could spend a weekend with me here in Vannetta? There's a spare room, and you wouldn't have to worry about seeing CAREY CROSS once. I'd be glad to have you as a guest anytime."

I folded the letter and placed it in the envelope. "Betty's really off her perch this time."

My mother shrugged, and even Marcia was silent.

It was a warning, this letter of Betty's. I just knew something bad was going to happen. Maybe I'd flip, dress up in RACHEL's little Daisy Mae sundress, put a bow in my hair and hop a bus to Vannetta.

"I don't want to see any more letters from Betty," I said

as I began tearing the pink envelope into little pieces, slowly, methodically.

"Okay," Marcia replied.

I didn't have to work on Monday, so I just stayed around the house in the morning, catching up on schoolwork and generally moping around. Now that my father was starting to perk up, I was taking his place as the family's gloomy gus. All day I promised myself I wouldn't watch the show. I watched the morning movie, one of my favorites. *Once More With Feeling* starring Yul Brynner, and even that didn't cheer me up.

At noon, I fixed an egg salad sandwich, ate half and wrapped the other half in plastic wrap for later. I didn't even feel like eating.

At one, I looked at the clock and imagined everyone would be preparing for the dress rehearsal.

At one-thirty, I tried to think of anything I could do that would take an hour and a half.

At one-fifty-six, our lead-in, CENTRAL RECEIVING, the medical soap, went off the air and I turned on the set. There was a commercial for detergent, one for panty hose and two spots plugging prime time shows. As the theme music came on, I almost stood up to turn the set off, but I remained on the couch.

First came the teaser, MILES discussing his imminent divorce with JANICE. VIOLET advising her daughter, LISA, not to rush into a relationship so soon after her husband, DEREK's, death. And CAREY CROSS receiving a supply of pills from STAN, the errand boy of mob boss, LOUIE QUARANTELLO.

I watched as LISA told VIOLET she had to put the bad experiences with DEREK behind her. Then JANICE explained to MARY just how intolerable life with MILES was.

Then we had some more commercials and opened to a scene with ALISON pleading for pills from CAREY. Strictly glycerin tears ran down her face as she screamed and threw a tantrum. Deanna couldn't cry on cue. Neither could I, but then I wasn't planning to be a star and she was, so the least she could do was produce genuine tears.

Then we switched back to MILES in the hospital, sharpening his scalpel on a razor strop. Not really, but he might as well have been honing it on a grinding stone for all the surgical technique he possessed.

Then RACHEL was working in the cafeteria after school, and various people bopped in to say hello.

Two thirty-one, more commercials.

Then back to the cafeteria. RACHEL was straightening things up when CAREY CROSS walked in.

"Hi, RACHEL."

"Gee, hi CAREY. What are you doing at the hospital?"

"Visiting you, darlin'. Think you can take a break?"

"Sure, I guess."

There was a special corner of the cafeteria used for private conversations. That's all people did in Riverford. Eat and talk.

"WOODIE's getting very concerned about ALISON," RACHEL said.

"Why?"

"She's been acting strangely, wild, staying up all night, sleeping all day. Have you noticed anything unusual?"

"ALISON's a very high-strung girl," CAREY said choosing his words carefully.

"WOODIE blames you."

"Me?" CAREY was instantly on the alert, defensive.

"He says you're too wild for her and she's changed since she's been dating you."

"WOODIE doesn't like me, so it's natural he'd blame me for whatever goes sour with ALISON."

"He says the family will be very upset if ALISON wants to marry you, and they'll do everything they can to prevent it."

CAREY smiled wryly. "Maybe they'll disown her the way they did my mother."

"I don't understand, CAREY, what are you talking about?"

He leaned back in his seat and looked at RACHEL for a moment, composing his thoughts. "My mother met a man, BRONTE CROSS, and fell in love with him. Her father said he'd disown her if she married him because BRONTE wasn't up to the REYDELS' social standing; the family had an image to maintain. Even though BRONTE CROSS was everything the REYDELS weren't, my mother was torn between love for him and love for her father. So she pleaded and begged with her father not to be angry, not to stop loving her, but told him that she was in love and wanted to be married. She was pregnant. But did her father take her in his arms? No. He threw her out of the house. She married my father . . ." CAREY paused and his eyes began to glisten. "And for the rest of his lifetime, my mother tried to help him, but every business venture he had failed and we never had anything. We lived in one-room apartments in Houston in the middle of the summer with no air conditioning because we couldn't afford the electric bill. We lived in Maine, in Seattle, in towns and cities all over the country, where my father thought he could find the fortune my mother had given up for him." CAREY wiped the tears away, not glycerin ones. He could cry on cue. "My grandfather never spoke with her again and polluted everyone's mind against us. When we came back to town, her own brother, EDWIN REYDEL, turned his back on her. Of course WOODIE would blame me for anything that happens to ALISON; they hate us. But whatever happens to ALISON is her own fault. She makes her own decisions."

The camera switched from CAREY's face to RACHEL's, which brimmed with compassion. She placed her hand on CAREY's.

Then we switched back to MILES, upstairs, scrubbing up for another butcher session in the O.R.

I sniffed back my own tears. Fitch was so good and so convincing that it gave me chills.

The phone rang, and I considered not answering it. Whoever it was, I didn't want to talk to them. But I reached for the receiver anyway.

"Hello?"

"Kate."

It was Fitch. "Hi. I was just watching the show."

"Yeah, it's on now. I just had a talk with Roxanne and Gene. They're buying out my contract."

"Why!"

"They said the show needs a dramatic event, and CAREY CROSS is going to give it to them."

"How?"

"He'll get killed. Somehow."

"When's this going to happen?"

"Next Friday."

"That's not even two weeks."

"When they want to get rid of you, they don't wait. I thought you'd want to know."

"The show will be nothing without CAREY! How can they be so stupid? I can't believe they're doing this!"

"They're the producers and we're expendable so they can do it. I've got to get back to the set. I'll talk to you tomorrow, okay?"

"Sure." We didn't even say goodbye. We just hung up.

Sure. Everything was fine and dandy. Peachy keen. My banquet had just gone into the trash bin.

Seventeen

ON TUESDAY, MY FATHER DROVE into the city with me to talk
to Sylvia. She had been telling him for the past two months
that there were plenty of jobs out there if he would only come
down and see about them. As we drove past the Westchester
County airport, a small corporate jet with red, white and
green lights flashed over our heads. Then we turned off
toward White Plains.

"Kate, I know you're upset about Fitch. I feel as if I
should be able to say something . . ."

"I know. There's nothing to say."

"You really think he'll go back to the coast?"

"Well, let's see. If we finish taping at five, he'll make the
seven o'clock flight to LAX. Yes, he'll go back."

"Look, I know L.A. is three thousand miles away, but
that's not very far any more."

"It could be a million miles. Once he goes, our lives will
change. He'll get another job, and I'll stay here. In the beginning, we'll call or write, and then the spaces in between
will get longer until we only exchange Christmas cards. And
then maybe someday, if I'm lucky, I'll be in L.A. and I'll see
him. He'll look at me and say something like 'Don't I know
you from someplace? This isn't a line, but you look familiar
to me.'"

My father began laughing. "I'm sorry, Kate, but you do
have a way of putting things. He'll never forget you."

"Well maybe he won't forget me, but he'll forget to think
about me."

"What if you forget to think about him?"

Not likely. But what did I know? I didn't understand anything that was going on anyway. Maybe it was sort of like having an allergy. My mother only sneezed in the presence of ragweed. Once the ragweed was gone, she forgot there was such a thing as allergies. Maybe once Fitch was gone, I could think of other things.

Over the radio I could hear the first notes of our song. I never thought I'd have an our song with anyone; but there it was, and well on its way to becoming a hit. "Set You Free" was played at least once every time I got into the Jeep. "As close as I feel to you, It just can't go on like this, So I'll stand back and set you free, I only want to know just one thing, where the hell does that leave me?" I reached over and twisted the knob so I wouldn't have to listen.

"RACHEL and CAREY's theme," my father mused. "How'd they happen to choose it?"

"The network owns the record company. It was a new release, and Roxanne liked it. If they knew Whelan and Fitch were related, I'm sure they would have cancelled the whole idea. Maybe scrapped his recording contract, too."

"I don't think they'd go that far. Fitch says it's just professional differences, nothing more. He and Lavinia can't come to terms on CAREY. She resents the changes he's made."

"Dave makes the changes."

"Because Fitch suggests them."

"So let them fire Lavinia," I shot back.

"She's family. His three months can't compare with her eight years, so he'd be the one to go. See, Kate, you have to try to understand how the system works. Everyone has to get along together. Its like a garden. The producer is the gardener on the lookout for weeds to pluck before they begin to take over."

"Fitch isn't trying to take anything over, he's just trying

118

to do his job the best way he knows how."

"That's what you don't understand. All it takes is one person standing up and saying that maybe things don't have to be done exactly the way they come down. It's a threat to the system."

"Maybe the end product would be a little better if actors had some input."

He laughed. "Now you're beginning to think like an actor, but that's not how it works. At least not on this level."

We drove past Yonkers Raceway; the track was lit, but there were no horses trotting around.

"Kate, I know this is very upsetting to you, but it happens all the time. Don't worry about Fitch. He's talented and will find something else soon. Getting fired from LIFE isn't going to be held against him, because people with his kind of experience are always in demand. I guarantee he'll land on his feet."

I didn't say anything for the rest of the drive, didn't think much of anything, just had the sound of Whelan Cooper singing in my head.

We parked the car and went into the studio together since he had an hour to wait before his breakfast date with Sylvia.

"This is strange, coming back after all these months," he said as we walked past the guard. "I never expected to come back, even for a visit."

Then people began greeting him, slapping him on the back, asking all kinds of questions, and I just left him there to talk to his friends. After being on the show for five years, it was natural he'd be considered part of the family. I was still an outsider and had never really tried to develop friendships with most of the cast. I had kept to myself, to Fitch; and the easy camaraderie Kerwin had with the cast made me feel isolated.

But more than Fitch made my problem: I was being

singled out. This was an ensemble company with everyone being equal. Except suddenly some of us were equaler, like Orwell's pigs. Deanna, Pete, Ellin and I had been placed in a mini-spotlight, and everyone's attention was now focused on us. It had nothing to do with us in particular; it was just a last ditch, desperate attempt to save the show. No one person mattered, only the show mattered. It had a life of its own. Yet being focused on made me different.

I smiled to myself as I walked into my dressing room. That was a good title for a new soap. LIFE OF ITS OWN. The continuing saga of . . .

"Hey, Kate?" Fitch poked his head in the door.

"Hi."

"Got a couple of minutes?"

"Sure, come on in."

"I saw your dad. He's the center of attention downstairs."

"It's his favorite place to be." I looked at him closely. "Why are you so happy?"

"I made some calls back to L.A. yesterday after I spoke to you, and I got a call last night."

"Yeah?" Why was I so leery, so suspicious?

"It's a great opportunity. I'm going to play Lucentio in *The Taming of the Shrew,* which will be presented at the Mark Taper Forum in May. John Urban has known me for a couple years and always wanted me to do something for him, but I was always busy. Then he was casting *Shrew* and learned I am rapidly on my way to becoming unemployed, so he gave me a call."

I didn't say anything for a moment. Certainly I wasn't shocked into silence. It was something akin to being struck dumb.

"It's something I've been wanting to do. I guess just about every actor wants to do Shakespeare."

"My father played Benedict at Stratford for a couple of weeks one summer."

"*Much Ado About Nothing.* Good part."

"He loved it. I'm really glad for you. I'm sure you're going to have a super time."

"I promised I'd see Roxanne early, so I'll catch you later."

"Sure. No problem."

He left.

"Brother," I said to myself in the mirror. "Did he ever land on his feet fast."

I got through the first reading of the script without realizing much of what was happening. If Lavinia pointed at me and told me to move, I did. All I kept wondering was how much I was worth?

Was I interchangeable, too. Could RACHEL be played by anyone, or was I specific to the character? It was obvious that Fitch had brought something to CAREY that couldn't be duplicated or they would have just let Fitch go and replaced him with another actor. It had been the same way with DEREK. My father had so carefully defined the character that it was impossible for another actor to come in and take over the part. So they killed him. And they were going to kill CAREY for the same reason. As actors they had just been too good.

How about RACHEL? How much was RACHEL worth in ratings points? How was my TV-Q, the measurement of Kathleen Rafferty's popularity and recognizability? Did I count at all?

At ten we left the rehearsal hall to go to breakdown. I walked up the backstairs and went down the hallway to Roxanne's office. I knocked on the door.

"Yes?"

I opened the door. "Do you have a few minutes?"

"Sure, Kate, come on in."

I guess my smileless face told her I was there on business. "What's on your mind?"

I didn't sit down. Once you sit, the scene tends to become

static. I had learned that from Fitch. He could move around the set, adding tension and drama to the weakest scene. "I can't say as I'm real happy with the way things are going around here."

"I'm sorry to hear that. What exactly is upsetting you?"

"Just let's say I'm upset about everything."

"Costumes?"

"Sure, costumes. RACHEL's dressed better, but she's still a wimp."

"Dialogue?"

"Sure. She gets some of the craziest lines to say. Sometimes I have to spend twenty minutes deciphering them. You people have to realize that some things can only be said on the typewriter. They can't be spoken by the human mouth."

"Is it Fitch?"

"Is what Fitch?"

"The fact that he'll be leaving. I know you've been pretty close to him. Kate, I'm sorry. I fought for him. I wanted him. I like him. I was the one who wanted him killed because no one can take his place. He made CAREY CROSS and I think Gene and Lavinia made a mistake, but please, don't repeat this to anyone or it'll cost me my job, if not my career."

"He's the only character with any spirit. Everyone else just drags around. Boring. WOODIE is boring, too sweet, and there's nothing behind him. Did you see the show the day CAREY told RACHEL about his mother?"

Roxanne nodded.

"He's a class act. And you people kick him out. I'm just really furious. You know, Roxanne, I didn't want this job to start with. I took it to help my father because you people let him go. I just want to get back to my normal life. This is craziness. I'm up before dawn, driving over a hundred and seventy miles round trip just to be here and mumble my way through some idiotic dialogue. Some people think this is their life, and they love it. My father loves it. I don't. I'm not an actress. I never wanted to be, and nothing has changed my mind."

"You may not have wanted to be an actress, but much has changed. You are an actress and becoming a very good one." Roxanne took a deep breath and folded her hands on top of her desk. "Your contract is coming up for renegotiation."

"You people can take that contract and hang it out in the wind. I don't care."

"Uh . . . wait a minute. You're going a little too fast, Kate."

"I'm not going fast enough. Watch me leave."

"Hold on for a minute. Sit down, please."

I sat reluctantly in a chair at the side of her desk. If you sit opposite someone behind their desk, it gives them a feeling of power over you. I learned that from Fitch.

"What would make you change your mind?"

"Nothing."

"I'd have to discuss this with Gene, but what do you want? You can have a limo if the driving's too much."

I practically laughed. "That's not it, Roxanne."

"Vacation time?"

"No."

"Okay, listen. Three days a week."

They wanted me.

"Roxanne, no."

"I can't bring back CAREY. I just can't do that."

"Okay," I was going to go for the wildest shot I could imagine. I was going to make them say no to me, no matter what Sylvia or my mother and father thought. I wanted out. "I want you to bring in a character for me."

"Okay."

"I want DEREK SIMMON's twin brother to land in Riverford."

"You want us to hire your father again?"

"Yes and for whatever money Sylvia asked for."

Roxanne gulped. "I don't have the power to do that."

I stood. "I understand. You just explain the situation to whoever it needs to be explained to and then let me know. Okay?" I walked out without waiting for her reply. I was as good as a civilian again. They'd never give in. I didn't smile, but I felt a whole lot better.

Eighteen

"I DON'T WANT TO SEE YOU AGAIN."

"Of course you do."

"I'll make sure I stay as far away from you as I can, and I want you to promise you'll do the same. Promise me that."

"I can't do that, RACHEL," CAREY told her.

"You have to. My father doesn't want me to see you."

"But you're a big girl, RACHEL. Are you going to do what he tells you to do for the rest of your life, or are you going to do what you want?"

"This is what I want," RACHEL said as she paced back and forth in her father's office at the hospital. "I don't want to see you. At all."

"You don't have to lie to me, RACHEL," CAREY said as he took a step closer to her, cornering her against her father's desk.

"I'm not lying!"

"You're just afraid to grow up," he said softly then kissed her.

RACHEL squirmed out of his arms and ran out the door.

"Okay, that's a take," Lavinia called over the intercom. "See you all tomorrow."

I walked back to the front of the set, exhausted. This day had been just a little too long.

"That was a really nice touch, Kate," Fitch said.

"What was."

"How RACHEL compulsively straightened her clothes,

pulling at the collar, pulling the sleeves down. Nice bit, really."

I didn't remember it.

My father approached. "I'm impressed. That was a good sequence."

We all walked out of the studio and into the hall. All I wanted was to get home. Since lunch I'd had a splitting headache, as if someone had tied a rope around my head and spent all afternoon gradually tightening it.

Roxanne came down the stairs. "Hi."

I nodded.

"Do you think you have a few minutes, Kate?" she asked.

"I'm really tired. Can it wait?"

"It'll just take a minute."

"I'll bring the car around," my father offered.

"I'll see you tomorrow, Kate," Fitch said, and they both walked away.

I started toward my dressing room. I wasn't even going to take off my make-up; I was just going home.

"I had a talk with Gene and Paula Sivertsen at the network this afternoon and I explained the situation to them as you explained it to me this morning."

Just tell me RACHEL is going to have emergency surgery and MILES lets the scalpel slip. I was praying hard.

"Have you any suggestions for what DEREK's brother's name should be?"

"What?" I almost shouted.

"There's a condition, though."

Well, there had to be.

"You have to sign for two years. We'll take your father for the same."

From the fog I had been in all day, my mind began to clear. "This is a bonus, not including an increase in money or any other perks Sylvia might negotiate."

"That's right. We want you as RACHEL, and we're

prepared to make some concessions in order to keep the momentum of the show. I say some, and I hope none of our other new people become unrealistic about what they can expect from us. After all, this is an ensemble company. There are no stars."

"So you all keep saying. Why don't you try telling that to DANIELLE and ALISON. It's wasted on me because I don't want to be a star, and I promise I'll resist all attempts to make me one. Do you understand?"

"Yes, Kate. You'd prefer not to have publicity."

"That's right. I just want to do my job. I'm being paid to act, is that right?"

"Your job is acting and helping the show. You're not going to be able to avoid it all."

"You see what you can do, all right?"

She nodded.

I took my sheepskin coat and pocketbook from my dressing room. "When the papers are ready, I'll take a look at them." I walked back down the hall to the door. It wasn't supposed to work this way. I was supposed to be a free woman. I had demanded the impossible, and they have given it to me.

Maybe I should have asked for a Caribbean island.

The next week and a half went by without my noticing much. I studied the scripts and did the scenes. RACHEL was in a constant frenzy, caught between MILES, WOODIE and CAREY. Everyone wanted something different from her, and she couldn't make up her mind which path she wanted to follow. WOODIE was in a frenzy, too, because ALISON's behavior was more bizarre every day from the pills. CAREY was pretty much in a frenzy as well, because LOUIE QUAR-ANTELLO wanted about ten thousand dollars in payment for pills, but CAREY had managed to spend the money instead. STAN was putting the squeeze on him. MILES wanted RACHEL to stay away from CAREY, since he was such a terrible influence; and the police were staking CAREY out, since everyone knew he was involved with the mob and illegal activities.

I had to force myself to get out of bed on Friday morning. I felt as if I hadn't slept in days. But I had because every night I dreamed that RACHEL was crying. It was a dream because RACHEL had never shed a tear. And as I drove down to the city, the sun cracking open the sky with watery yellow streaks, I still didn't have a script in my hand. Dave had written most of the scenes, but the final sequences with CAREY were a secret to those involved.

I guess if I'd had the energy, I'd have made a fuss. Luckily I was a quick study, but it was insane to expect anyone to get to the set and do the thing cold. Maybe Dave hadn't figured it out yet. The only thing I could hope was that during the next two years, Dave would get some kind of book in his head and be able to plan the story line out at least a few months in advance.

My father was thrilled there would soon be a DIRK SIMMONS in the world. I was glad I had been able to do that much for him. He had turned down an offer to do a summer package-show, *The Marriage Go-Round,* I think it was or maybe *Under The Yum-Yum Tree.* Those old summer favorites couldn't compare with being back in Riverford again, where he'd try to get involved with LISA once more. The cast and crew were delighted to hear they'd have him back again. TV *Guide* was going to run a little blurb in the news column about how LIFE would have a father-daughter act. My father's dream had come true.

Roxanne wondered if maybe DIRK couldn't prove to be RACHEL's father after an appropriate time, which would really stir Riverford up and infuriate MILES in the bargain. Or maybe it was DEREK who was RACHEL's father, or maybe it was DIRK who died, and DEREK and he had changed places and now DEREK was the one who was back. Just to have my father back gave them unlimited and incredibly complex possibilities.

The guard nodded to me as I came in the building and met Ellin coming down the stairs.

"Wait till you see the script!"

"Why?"

"You're going to kill CAREY!"

"I thought the mob was going to put him down. Concrete kimono time."

She shook her head and handed me her script. "Page seventy-five."

I flipped through the pages until I found the place. Sure enough RACHEL was going to kill CAREY. Maybe that was another condition Roxanne hadn't mentioned. Just a nudge of retribution in my ribs, to keep me in line. The producers giveth and the producers taketh away.

"WOODIE is slipped some drug into his coffee by CAREY and flips out. When RACHEL finds out, she goes on the warpath, in case you're wondering why RACHEL kills her beloved CAREY. MILES says he doesn't know if WOODIE will pull through, and RACHEL goes to CAREY's apartment to tell him just what a creep he is."

"Terrific." I sat down in my dressing room chair. Whoever was looking back at me out of the mirror looked terrible. Not yet eighteen years old, and I felt as if the bloom was off my youth. Was I going to have to start frequenting Elizabeth Arden's salon for facials with Elisa and Deanna?

"Hi, Ellin. Could I speak with Kate?" Fitch asked as he stepped into the room.

"Sure, no problem," she said and left.

"See the script?" he asked.

I nodded.

"A twist of fate. Or a twist of David's mind." He paused. "I'm leaving on an early flight tomorrow morning; I need to get the business about *Shrew* lined up. And there are a couple of other things I need to look into."

My chest felt something like the time I had fallen out of my treehouse and had the wind knocked out of me. I couldn't breath for about a minute, and it seemed like forever.

"I wanted you to have this." He handed me a record album. I saw the name on the cover. Whelan Cooper "Fear of the Past" featuring his new hit song "Set You Free." Whelan looked like Fitch, though his hair was darker, more sandy colored; but the bone structure was the same. They were unmistakably brothers.

"He's on tour now, out in Michigan, but he'll be back in a month to keep me company at home for a couple weeks before he goes again."

I knew they shared a house in Malibu, on the ocean. Between the two of them, they could afford just about anything. I didn't know why Fitch had ever left L.A. when everything for him was on the coast. He had been born there, his parents were there, his house was there. Probably all kinds of friends, of both genders.

"I'm guess I'm saying goodbye now."

I guess he was.

"For someone else, getting fired from this job probably would have been pretty devastating, but I want you to know that I feel it was a positive experience for me. I don't regret any time I spent here, because I spent it with you. I think you're going to do well in this business, and I don't want you to underestimate what you have to offer. Once you tap into your natural resources, you'll see for yourself how much talent you have. It'll happen for you."

When I was eighty-eight and if I was living at the Motion Picture Home, I would look back on my career, even if I had won five Oscars, and never believe I had talent. I would think I had always been lucky and had just gotten by. And had learned the most from some blond guy with a funny name that I couldn't remember anymore. Because I knew in my heart, I was never going to see him again. At least not in real life. In time, it would all fade, like scripts and dialogue of the past, like characters coming in and out of a serial. To remember, would be like the thrust of a stilletto. I knew what Whelan Cooper was singing about. But even that would go. I didn't know what came next. Maybe someday I'd be driving to work, past the Stella D'Oro bakery, and Whelan's new song would play on my radio and he'd have the answer for me. I know I didn't have it.

"I hope you do well as Lucentio," I said. I couldn't ask him to give me a call and tell me how it went for him because it was all over. I didn't want him to feel that I was grasping at him, to feel responsible for keeping in touch with me. More than three thousand miles would be separating us; it was better to end it now, cleanly, in one shot, then to let it bleed slowly to death.

"Come on, Kate. Let's do it one last time and make it so good no one who sees it will ever forget how CAREY and RACHEL were together."

Nineteen

"You slipped some drug into WOODIE's coffee, didn't you?"

"What if I did?"

"You did, didn't you? Why don't you admit it!" RACHEL shouted.

"All right, I did!"

"Why? WOODIE never did anything to you!"

"He didn't?" CAREY slammed his fist down on his desk. "He's been getting everything that should have been mine all these years. I never had anything. He had it all. And then he had you."

"Me?"

"Sure. When I came to town, I thought you were a silly kid and if I had to get you away from WOODIE to hurt him, I would."

"You were using me!"

"Only in the beginning! Only in the beginning . . . RACHEL, you believed in me. You cared about me. No one's ever cared about me before. And still WOODIE had you. You were turning away from me, and I need you!"

"But you tried to kill him!"

"I had to!" CAREY brushed his arm across the top of the desk, smashing the lamp to the floor. "Do you have any idea of how much money I owe? These people won't wait. I can't stall them off any longer."

"What does that have to do with WOODIE?"

"RACHEL, don't you know anything? EDWIN REYDEL is the District Attorney. He's been going after LOUIE

QUARANTELLO for years, and it's getting too hot. They told me to stop my uncle; WOODIE was supposed to be a warning. I didn't give him enough to kill him, just enough to put him down for a while."

"CAREY, this is craziness. You've got to get out."

"I can't get out, I'm in too far. You've got to stay with me, RACHEL. Help me, I need you."

"I can't," RACHEL said as she pulled her arm out of his grasp. "I can't. I've got too much to lose."

"You love me, RACHEL. You want me."

"I don't. I love WOODIE."

"You don't love WOODIE, you just wish you did. He doesn't need you, and you're the kind of girl who needs to be needed."

"I need security. I can't get it with you."

"But I love you," CAREY told her and put his arm around her, then began kissing her.

"CAREY, stop. Let me go."

"RACHEL, please. Stay with me."

"I can't! Let me go!"

He kissed her again, and she began to struggle against him. With a shove, she pushed him away. He stumbled back over the coffee table and fell against the corner of his very expensive stereo speaker. It was his tweeters and woofers that did him in.

RACHEL stood there for a moment and stared. "CAREY?" she asked. There was no answer. "Oh my God. CAREY?" She took a step closer to him. He didn't move. She gulped hard then knelt down alongside him. "CAREY? Are you all right?" RACHEL asked as the tears began to well up in her eyes. "CAREY . . . wake up, please." She shook him lightly by the shoulder. "You've got to be all right. Wake up. Oh God. CAREY! God, he's dead. I killed him." RACHEL started to panic, tears streaming down her face. "What am I going to do? I can't be found here. I'll

133

be sent to jail. I didn't kill him. It was just an accident. I didn't mean to do it. CAREY, wake up." She shook him hard, then slowly leaned over. "Oh no, he's not breathing. He's dead. What am I going to do. Somebody's going to find me here. I've got to get away. I'm sorry. I'm sorry. I didn't mean to do it. It was an accident. CAREY, believe me. I didn't mean to do it." RACHEL stood, rushed to the door, then looked around the room. It was in a shambles. She grabbed her pocketbook off the floor and ran out the door.

The next thing I heard was applause. The crew had liked what they'd seen.

I walked around the back of the flat, into the bright lights. Fitch was standing there, smiling at me.

"Nice work, RACHEL," the a.d. said.

The crew began to move the equipment, closing down for the day. People began to leave the set.

I stood there, for the last time in CAREY CROSS's apartment, as if to fix it in my memory.

"I told you that when you tapped your resources, you'd see how talented you are," Fitch told me.

How much of it was acting? How much was RACHEL? In true Riverford soap tradition, I had instant amnesia. I couldn't remember anything I had just done.

I woke up early the next morning because I was used to getting up at five, sat up in bed and waited for the first light. Then I studied the crack in the wall, the one produced by the settling foundation. I wondered if he was up, then I wondered if he was putting on his coat, then I wondered how he was getting out to the airport. By seven-thirty I knew he was at the airport and by eight I knew he had left. Somehow then it was really over and I felt better, if it could be called better to be one step up from total desolation.

My mother called me for breakfast, and I went down to sit with them. My father was in a cheerful mood, looking forward to getting back to work in another week, speculating on how much of a dastard DIRK SIMMONS would be in comparison to DEREK. Everything seemed back to normal. We were back in the old routine. Nothing had changed, except we were both working now.

I schlepped over to Marcia's on the road, not through the fields. In the bedroom, her radio was on. Whelan Cooper again. That was practically all I ever heard anymore.

"How was it yesterday?"

"Not so bad. RACHEL pushed him into the stereo and he cracked his head. The end."

"Oh."

"Maybe I shouldn't have told you so you could have been surprised like everyone else."

"You violated the cardinal rule of not telling anyone what's going to happen."

I shrugged. With the way my luck kept backfiring, I'd probably receive a commendation from Gene if he found out.

"So Fitch left this morning."

"Yep."

"Well, Kate, you'll get over it."

"I'm sure I will. Just a scratch. Not even worth putting a Band-Aid on."

"Sure. You're in a position to meet a lot of people now."

I nodded. "True. And so can he."

"Right. So everything will work out. Be a little philosophical about it. If something was meant to happen, it would have happened. I know you felt really close to him, but maybe it was because he was out here alone and you were working for the first time with strangers, so you just gravitated to each other and that was all it was."

"Probably."

"You'll make other friends."

"You're beginning to sound like a mother."

"Maybe so, but I hate to see you dragging yourself around

over this. You've got everything going for you and . . . well, Kate, men are like fish. The ocean's full of them."

"I'm over it already." I smiled. "We were just good friends. What was in the mail this week?"

"Plenty," Marcia said as she began spreading the letters out on her desk.

I leaned over, resting my hand on the desk to study a drawing someone had sent me.

"Kate! Where's your ring?" Marcia asked suddenly.

I looked at my hand. "I guess I must have forgotten to put it on."

Twenty

"Do you think i killed CAREY?"

Ellin was lounging on FONDA's bed, glancing through the faked-up Riverford Sentinel, the newspaper that focused on a new murder suspect each week.

"I could have done it, you know," she continued.

I was sitting in FONDA's bedroom chair, a pink chintz thing, trying to catch up on my history. School would be over in six weeks, and I was forever trying to finish homework. Whether or not FONDA had killed CAREY was relatively unimportant in the face of final exams.

"FONDA liked CAREY all along, but since you worked your way with him. . . ."

"Your fingerprints weren't in the apartment. Only ALISON, HOPE, STAN and RACHEL are suspects," I replied.

"And MILES, who came there looking for RACHEL. The cops didn't look in the refrigerator. I was there. I had a can of beer while I was waiting for CAREY to come home. As I walked into the living room, aimlessly, I tripped over his body. A look of shock came over my face, close-up, take FONDA. Bridge to commercial." Ellin laughed.

"I thought you said you killed him, not found him."

"I could have. And I had reason. I was jealous of his relationship with ALISON. She's pregnant by him you know."

"So you say," I responded, knowing Marcia believed ALISON was pregnant by him, too.

"You haven't mentioned him in a while. How's Fitch doing? Have you heard from him lately?"

"I guess it was about two weeks ago. He called to say the rehearsals for *Shrew* were starting. I told him RACHEL is on the verge of a nervous breakdown what with this murder investigation going on and on and the one detective following her around trying to find out if she knows more than she's telling."

Ellin paused. "You still miss him then?"

I closed my history book. "Yeah, I still miss him. I still walk into the studio and look for him. And sometimes I can feel him with me."

"What do you mean?"

"When I'm out there, in the middle of a scene and it's just going along, it's as if he reaches out and touches me. Then I'm on a different level, in an entirely different place. It's just not the same. I don't know how to explain it."

Ellin sat up and slid herself over to the edge of the bed. "You know, Kate, when you came on the show, you couldn't act."

"I never said I could."

"You were uncomfortable and it was obvious, but in the past couple of months, it's all begun to come together for you. I might have to start getting jealous."

"I have so much to learn about the craft, and I want to learn, but I'm not sure I'll ever be satisfied."

"We all have a lot to learn, and once you get satisfied, you stop growing. That's what's so fantastic about acting, you just keep expanding; it doesn't ever have to stop."

"But I feel as though my ability is just a speck on the surface. When I watch my father, I wonder if I'll ever have his proficiency, his finesse. He's a professional; I'm still just goofing off."

Ellin shook her head. "Not anymore. You've joined the club, Kate. It's funny, but sometimes when I watch you, I'm

138

reminded of Fitch's style. In the past couple of months, I've seen your father, too. You're taking from both of them. And one day, I even saw Hugh in you."

"No!"

"Hugh's good."

"He's been a lot better since my father came back; now MILES doesn't pinch my fanny any more."

Jack paged us for taping, and I stood.

"You'll be okay today. Just do it."

I wondered. It was a tough scene, and I had known it was coming ever since DIRK SIMMONS had arrived in Riverford, much to everyone's surprise and annoyance. I had been on the same set with my father a number of times, but I had never really played a scene with him. I was as nervous and insecure as I would have been playing against a famous star; it didn't seem to matter much that it was my father.

JANICE crossed in front of me and stopped. "Don't be nervous, honey. It's hard the first time, but you'll be surprised how easy it is."

"Do I look that scared?"

She smiled broadly. "Something like Marie Antoinette on her way to the guillotine. I've known your father for years; he's lots of fun, and he'll make you feel comfortable. He's probably as nervous as you are."

"Impossible."

"Even we old fossils get nervous. This is a big scene for him, too."

"He's always so cool."

"He's been pacing in the hallway for about fifteen minutes. I'd love it if they'd write in a relationship between JANICE and DIRK, Kerwin's so much more fun than Hugh. Hugh just doesn't give anything back to you. Know what I mean?"

"RACHEL," Jack paged over the intercom. "You're wanted on the set. DIRK. Have you disappeared, too?"

My father stopped next to me, and we looked at each other for a moment. Then he kissed me lightly and went around back of the set.

In the luncheonette, where I first met CAREY, I sat down at the booth. I wanted to be good. I wanted my father to be proud of me, and I wanted to get through this scene without making a fool of myself.

"Roll tape."

RACHEL sat alone in the booth, staring at her hands, which gave Lavinia time to superimpose the sequence of CAREY and RACHEL's last confrontation. Tears came to RACHEL's eyes as she remembered CAREY falling and hitting his head.

She glanced up, startled, as DIRK came to stand next to her.

"May I sit down?" he asked.

She shrugged.

He sat across from her. "Did you know my brother, DEREK?"

"No. He died before I came to Riverford."

"Do you know anything about him?"

"No, not really."

"You just know he was a scoundrel."

I looked at him in surprise, almost as if I had been standing knee deep in the ocean and a wave had just crashed into me. It was DIRK sitting in the booth across from me. It didn't even look like my father anymore. "I don't know if I believe gossip; I like to make my own decisions," RACHEL replied. "Besides, DEREK's dead."

"Just like your friend, CAREY CROSS. I've heard you were close to him."

"I wasn't. We were just casual friends. I didn't really know him at all."

"RACHEL, you don't have to lie to me. I know you."

"You don't know me at all. I've only seen you at the hospital a few times."

DIRK reached over and put his hand on RACHEL's hand. "Did you ever wonder why JANICE is so cold to you? I've seen how she treats you."

"She's taken me into her house. I'm a stranger, an intruder to her."

"JANICE knows the truth, because JANICE knows who I am."

"What truth? What does JANICE know?"

"RACHEL, you're so pretty."

RACHEL tried to stand up and leave the booth, but he grabbed her wrist and wouldn't release his grip. "Let me go."

"I let you go once and that was the biggest mistake of my life."

"I don't know what you're talking about." RACHEL was starting into one of her famous panics. "I have to go. Please. Let me go."

"RACHEL, sit down." When she didn't, he tightened his grip, until she did as he said. "Why do you think MILES hates me so much?"

"I don't think he does. He's just as shocked as everyone else that DEREK had a twin brother."

"No he's not shocked. He's known me for years. For many years. I dated . . . I was in love with CONSTANCE before she ever met MILES. But I wasn't wealthy, and she was a girl who needed money."

"My mother wasn't like that."

"She was when I knew her."

"I don't believe any of this."

"She chose MILES over me, but that didn't mean she gave me up. You're my daughter."

RACHEL shook her head. "You're lying. MILES is my father."

"I am your father, and you'd better learn to accept that."

"No, I'll never accept that. My mother wouldn't do that. She wouldn't pass off another man's child as her husband's, even if she had left him. She wouldn't have done that."

"She did do exactly that, RACHEL. Where do you think she got your name?"

"I don't know."

"My mother's name was RACHEL."

"You're lying. Nothing you say is the truth. I don't know why you're making this story up, but it's not going to get you anyplace."

"CONSTANCE was always in love with me. And even after she was married to MILES, she wanted me."

RACHEL wrenched her arm from DIRK's grasp. "I'll never believe you. I hate you. I *hate you* for saying those things about my mother!" RACHEL screamed and raced from the set.

I stood there for a moment, making the transition from RACHEL to Kate and realized my father had been right all along. Acting with someone you loved was different, special.

He came around the back of the set. "Have I ever told you how glad I am you're my daughter?"

I put my arms around him and hugged him tight. "Did you feel it?"

"Yes. Did you?"

"Yes." It was like being in perfect harmony. But I'd felt it before. "I'm going to take a flight to L.A. Saturday."

"When did you decide that?"

"Just now. It's unfinished business."

"I thought you might have gotten over him."

"I guess not."

"It's pretty radical; can't you just call him?"

"This has to be done in person."

"Are you going to call him first, let him know you're coming?"

I shook my head. "No."

"That's a mistake. I don't think it's a good idea to surprise him."

"Why. Because I don't know what I'll find? Maybe I'll be more surprised then he is?"

"Something like that."

"It's something I have to do."

"If you've got your mind made up, there's nothing I can say but good luck. I hope it works out."

"Yeah, me, too."

Twenty-one

I PICKED MY TICKET and boarding pass and walked to the end of the concourse where my flight was to take off. I would have preferred first class because sitting with my knees practically up to my chest for four or five hours in tourist wasn't very appealing. But I was lucky to get a seat at all because it was the beginning of spring vacation for most schools in the metropolitan area. I hadn't known that. I didn't know much of anything that was happening in the outside world anymore.

Because I was early, I had to sit in the lounge and wait, nothing to do but listen to the whine of jet engines and watch people schlep carry-on luggage around the terminal. I had my bag by my seat. Clothes for one day, just one change. I had to be back by Sunday night or I'd never make the Monday show.

The longer I sat there, the crazier the plan seemed to be. I was flying six thousand miles, ten hours at least on a plane, plus four hours traveling time to my home, plus whatever it would take to get from the airport in L.A. to Malibu. Just for what. To say hello?

Why was I doing this?

I was feeling a taste of RACHEL's panic well up in my throat and almost picked up my bag to walk back to the counter and cancel the whole deal, when my flight was announced. Along with everyone else, I boarded the plane, found my seat on the aisle, and settled myself down. I opened a book I was supposed to read for school but couldn't concentrate with all the people walking down the aisle next to me.

A mother and daughter paused in front of my seat, checked their ticket and began to settle themselves down across from me. The daughter looked at me briefly, then turned away, then looked at me again. A classic doubletake. She whispered to her mother, and then her mother turned to look at me.

The flight attendant came past, instructing everyone to fasten their seatbelts, and soon the plane was pulling away from the building. There was no going back now. The next time I'd touch ground, it would be in L.A. Of course, I could stay at LAX and catch the next flight back to New York. I wondered if I had lost my mind. My mother said I had. My father encouraged me to go if it was something I had to do; God, I loved him. And I was so glad he was working again; it made him a different person: happy, fulfilled, satisfied, his old hammy self.

"Excuse me," the flight attendant said as she leaned over to me. "I'm just wondering, do you play RACHEL FERGUSON on LIFE TO ITS FULLEST?"

"Yes, I confess, I do."

"Oh, Mom. I was right! It is her!" The girl sitting across from me exclaimed.

"I watch the show whenever and wherever I can," the flight attendant continued. "I'm just curious to know if RACHEL did kill CAREY CROSS. I thought she might have stunned him and someone else entered the apartment after she left and really did the job."

These seeds of doubt had been planted more than a month ago and had stirred up a storm of controversy. Dave was milking the idea without having anyone actually say that that might have been the case. I didn't know what the final outcome was going to be, but as far as I was concerned RACHEL had done the black deed.

I smiled.

"I know you can't say anything. I just want you to know how much we all like the show. It's our favorite. I used to think of it as my mother's show. The characters were all older, VIOLET and FRED HEGARTY and TRAVERS and ODETTE; but in the past few months, it's been really interesting."

"I'm glad you like it," I replied.

"Oh I do. And you're such a good actress. Sometimes I cry right along with you. But I'd better get to the kitchen and begin serving lunch. I'd like to speak with you later, if you don't mind."

"Sure, no problem."

The woman left, and the girl across from my seat, leaned over her mother. "Are you really RACHEL FERGUSON?"

"Sure. I'm really RACHEL." Why not?

"I adore WOODIE. When are you guys going to get married?"

I laughed. "I think that might be a long way off yet. WOODIE has to finish school first."

"Is ALISON going to have CAREY's baby?"

"I don't know. ALISON is having a difficult time making up her mind."

"Well, it is getting a little late, isn't it?" the mother asked. "She can't very well have an abortion now."

Dave had that all figured out precisely so that ALISON would keep everyone guessing up until the last minute, which was in the middle of May. "You'd have to ask MILES about that, he's the doctor in the family."

"It must be a wonderful job," the mother said.

"It's very nice."

"And you get to play all those scenes with WOODIE," the girl said. I imagined her to be about my age, but she seemed younger. "That CAREY CROSS was so evil, I'm glad he's dead. I cheered when he fell against the stereo, leading RACHEL on that way, doing all those mean things to ALISON and then putting the drugs in WOODIE's coffee."

A flight attendant brought lunch, and I opened a pack of sugar to put in my tea.

"I don't think," the girl continued, "that the guy who played CAREY CROSS could have been a very nice person. Nobody could be that convincing and not be evil, too."

I stirred my tea and sighed. "You couldn't be more wrong," I told her. And at that moment missed him more sharply than I had at any time in the months since he had left. I wanted to act with him again, to feel close to him, to be myself with him.

The flight attendants were gathered at the doorway as I was about to leave the plane, and they all told me again how much they enjoyed the show and how much they enjoyed me as RACHEL. These were the people who made it possible for me to meet Fitch, to give me a job and my father a job and paid my way to L.A. that day. These women, and people like them, were the fans, and without them there would be no show. I thanked them and left.

Outside, in the heat, I flagged down a cab and gave him the address in Malibu. He told me it would take a while, and I leaned back in the seat to wait.

What if Fitch didn't come home at all, and I just waited for nothing? What if he came home with someone. I tried not to think about it, and instead just concentrated on the scenery. Welcome to America, Kate. It's all the same. Fast food joints, used car lots, shopping centers, rust and garbage, but in L.A. there were palm trees, pink buildings and Spanish castles and colonial houses and everything mixed in.

We got out by the ocean, and it was beautiful. I could smell the salt in the air.

"This address is in a really good neighborhood," the taxi driver told me as we drove along the coast.

147

"Is it?"

"Some relatives of yours?" he asked.

"Friends."

"They must be rich."

"Very rich, I suppose."

"In the industry?"

"Show business? Yes."

"I've got a screenplay I've been working on," he said warming to the topic. "Are these people in feature films?"

"No."

"TV movies?" he asked hopefully.

"No."

"Well, I've only had this job six weeks, and I know one day I'll pick up someone important. My friend picked up Tony Bill last week. You know who he is?"

"No."

"Big time producer. I wish I had been there at the airport for that one. But you never can tell, can you?"

"No, you can't."

"Someday I'll get my big break. You're a good-looking kid, you'll get your break, too, someday. Just keep plugging. You do want to be in the business, don't you? Be an actress?"

I thought about it for a moment. "Yes."

"Of course, everyone does. Well, you just stay out here. This is where it's all happening. L.A. is the entertainment capitol of the world. Where are you from, Ohio or something? Almost everyone who comes here is from Ohio."

"I'm from New York."

"Nothing's going on back there, better move here for good. Are you moving here now?"

"No, I'm just visiting."

"Oh taking a vacation. When are you leaving?"

"Tomorrow."

I could see him look up into his rearview mirror to see if I was kidding. "That's not much of a vacation."

"I'm taking care of unfinished business," I said.

"Oh." He slowed the taxi and stopped in front of a house. "Beautiful place. Must've cost plenty. You know what these beach houses go for?"

"No."

"Mega-bucks."

I gave him twenty dollars, told him to keep the change and stepped out.

The house was natural wood, with a small garden in front, eucalyptus and small palm trees covered the front. A redwood deck ran around the side of the house, and I could see the ocean and part of the beach. I went down the walk and knocked on the door. No answer. I walked around the side of the house until I reached the back patio, which overlooked the ocean. The rear wall of the house was entirely glass. I knocked again, but there was no answer. Since there were no cars out front, I guessed no one was home.

So I sat on a lounge chair, kicked off my shoes, and settled down to wait. Even if he wasn't planning to be home that night, he'd for sure come home to change before going out. Unless of course he'd left early that morning or Friday night for the weekend.

I decided I had truly lost my mind and this was the most insane thing I had ever done in my life; but instead of making me feel like a jerk, it made me feel good. For the past months, I'd been carried along like a feather on the water, never knowing where I was going to end up; things just kept happening so fast I couldn't deal with them. But this time I had the jump on everything. I had set the thing in motion, and I could wait to see what would happen.

The worst thing wouldn't be missing Fitch and going home without seeing him. The worst thing would be seeing him come home with another girl. It wasn't as though I didn't figure he'd have lady friends, but I just wanted them to be passing acquaintances. I didn't know how he felt about me, and I didn't know exactly how I felt about him. In a couple of months, I'd be eighteen, and I'd never been in love before. I didn't know what it was supposed to be like or if what I felt added up to that. I could be making something out of nothing; or it could be strictly one-sided. I wasn't thinking about next week or next month or next year, I just wanted to stand in front of him and see if I felt the same way now that I did the first time I saw him on the set. If the butterfly squadron scrambled into flight, then I'd know it wasn't just some fantasy I'd been having, that it was real, at least for me.

A couple of hours went by. I read and fell asleep, and when I woke, the sun was coming low toward the ocean. A glance at my watch told me it was almost five; I had packed enough food to sustain me for dinner; I was prepared. And if he didn't show up by ten, I'd just find a phone, call a taxi and get myself driven to the nearest motel for the night. I had everything figured out. I wasn't stranded.

Turning over, I watched the orange streamers of light rippling on the water, under an orangeade sky. I loved the ocean: the smell, the sound, the presence of it. Living up there in Connecticut was too calm. I wanted to live on the ocean and face the storms, with their crashing waves and lightning and thunder, and get soaking wet with spray. Once we had spent a summer in Maine, on the oceanfront in Bar Harbor, when my father was in summer stock. I had cut my toe on a shell and loved every minute of it.

"Hey, darlin' what are you doing here?" The sliding glass door opened, and Fitch stepped out onto the deck; he was followed by a huge Irish wolfhound who stuck her face in my face and began to lick. "Deirdre, where are your manners? Stop it." The dog turned to him, and duly chastised, stretched out on the deck.

I sat up and pushed the hair off my face. "I don't know."

"That's a pretty long trip to make not knowing."

I stood and looked behind him into the house to see if there was anyone else in there.

"Kate, where's your ring?" he asked as he reached for my hand.

"I stopped wearing it."

"Why?"

I paused. "I didn't know if I should. And it made me think of you."

"I gave it to you to wear. And what's wrong with thinking about me?"

"Fitch, I guess maybe I've led a sheltered life and maybe you saw that when you joined the show and decided I needed to be protected or befriended or something."

"You're the last person who needs to be protected. Nothing anyone says or does will make a difference to you. You'll go through life without being changed by any circumstances. In this business, that's more than unusual, it's practically unheard of."

"Maybe you're wrong. You made a difference to me. Maybe I'm dumb and inexperienced, but I've thought about this a lot, and I've figured it out the best I can. I guess I'm in love with you. Now I'm not expecting you to say anything in particular in response. I've just been living in limbo for the past couple of months because of this unfinished business between us. Because I didn't know about myself. Maybe I should have said something earlier, before you left, but I wasn't even sure today until you walked through the door. So now I can go back home."

"You came three thousand miles to make this little discovery, and then you're going to leave?"

I nodded.

"Want to go out to dinner? I haven't eaten since breakfast."

"You don't have other plans?"

"No." He smiled. "There's a nice restaurant down the

beach. We can walk there if you want."

"Sure. I've been sitting all day."

Fitch pushed Deirdre into the house and closed the sliding door behind her. "I've been rehearsing practically day and night the last couple of weeks, but I think we'll be ready. Watch the steps when you come down, they're very steep."

I followed him down the steps and onto the sand. I sank in over my feet. We began walking, his hands in his pockets, my hands in my pockets, silent for a while.

"I'm really proud of how you're coming along, Kate."

"What do you mean?"

"You're really getting to be a fine actress. A real natural."

I looked at him, questioningly.

"I caught the show when I could before rehearsals began. And since then, I've been taping it. I really miss acting with you. I really miss being with you."

"I kind of figured you would have found someone else to . . . uh, hang around with."

"Once you've had steak, hamburger isn't too appealing."

"What an outrageous thing to say!" But I had to smile anyway.

"You know anything about *The Taming of the Shrew?*"

"I saw the movie."

"Um . . . Lucentio has a short speech in Act 1. It always reminds me of you."

"Well, let's hear it."

> "O Tranio, till I found it to be true,
> I never thought it possible or likely.
> But see, while idly I stood looking on,
> I found the effect of love in idleness,
> And now in plainness do confess to thee,
> That art to me as secret and as dear
> As Anna to the Queen of Carthage was,

Tranio, I burn, I pine, I perish, Tranio,
If I achieve not this young modest girl.
Counsel me, Tranio, for I know thou canst.
Assist me, Tranio, for I know thou wilt."

I didn't say anything for a moment.

"Maybe I should have said something before I left, but I
didn't want to complicate things. I would rather have you as
a friend than not at all. I figured it was my imagination, that
all I was to you was a big brother. I was afraid you weren't
ready, that I wasn't ready. And I didn't want to stick around
and find out. Then I came out here and immediately got very
miserable."

"Fitch . . ."

We began to walk up the steps to the restaurant.

"I've got a tape my brother sent me a couple of weeks
back. You can have it. It'll be his new hit, I guess, and it was
written for me because I keep calling him around the country,
telling him how things are. He says I've got it bad."

"What's the song called."

" 'Three – Thousand – Mile, Long – Distance – Romance
Blues.' "

"I'm more than vaguely familiar with that affliction myself."

"Kate, do you have your ring with you?"

I took it out of my pocket.

"Will you wear it?"

I nodded.

The maitre d' came and showed us to a table.

"Will you come back and see me in the play?"

"Of course. Were you going to invite me out for the
opening?"

"What would have stopped me? I think the airlines are
going to get rich off of us."

153

"Ana the phone company."

"And the U.S. Postal Service."

A woman walked by the table then stopped and stared at me for a moment. "Excuse me," she said. "You look so much like Kathleen Rafferty from LIFE TO ITS FULLEST."

"I am Kate Rafferty."

"No," she said with a slightly puzzled expression. "Not quite, but close."

Fitch began laughing. I laughed along with him. Then he took the ring out of my hand and slipped it on my finger.

Cast of Characters

Kate Rafferty– plays RACHEL FERGUSON.

Kerwin Rafferty– Kate's father; ex-DEREK SIMMONS who had been married to LISA HEGARTY, daughter of FRED and VIOLET HEGARTY; then becomes DEREK SIMMONS' twin brother, DIRK.

Diana Rafferty– Kate's mother.

Fitch Cooper– plays CAREY CROSS, son of HOPE REYDEL CROSS and BRONTE CROSS.

Ellin Tierney– plays FONDA, daughter to LOUISE.

Peter Searle– plays WOODIE REYDEL, son of District Attorney EDWIN REYDEL, stepbrother to ALISON REYDEL.

Deanna Davison– plays ALISON REYDEL.

Miriam Stern– plays JANICE FERGUSON, stepmother of RACHEL.

Hugh Fitzgerald– plays MILES FERGUSON, father of RACHEL.

Grace Ransom– plays VIOLET HEGARTY, thus making her DEREK SIMMONS's mother-in-law.

Elisa Fairbairn– plays DANIELLE.

Marilyn Grimes– plays LOUISE, mother of FONDA.

MARGO REYDEL– mother of ALISON, stepmother of WOODIE.

STAN– intermediary between CAREY CROSS and the mob.

LOUIE QUARANTELLO– the mobster who had DEREK SIMMONS mugged.

Lavinia Dale-Crozier– director.
Dave Dietz– head writer.
Jack– assistant director.
Bill– stage manager.
Gene DeMeglio– producer.
Roxanne Devere– assistant producer.
Marcia Loesch– Kate's best civilian girlfriend.
Sylvia Greenberg– the Raffertys' agent.
Whelan Cooper– Fitch's brother.